One Simple Memory

Jean Kelso

ISBN: 978-0-9951929-2-8

I dedicate this book to my family, my mother, my sisters, and my father who is in heaven watching over me, without you I would not be here. To my loving husband who supports me through thick and thin and to my kids, I love you all.

Acknowledgments

Thank you to my wonderful betas, my Kinky Jems: Shannon, Tracey, Brittany, Amy, and Jessica. I appreciate you all more than you will ever know. We managed to do the hit and miss a lot in the group because of the time zones, but I thank you all for everything.

A special thank-you goes out to Beth Michelle Luciano for taking the time out of her busy life of writing her own book to review mine. For the constant bugging you tolerated from me and for still being kind and supportive no matter what—you amaze me. For encouraging me and supporting me along the way.

Casey Harvell, Measha Stone, and Tonya Ridener for all the original works when I first published. You all rock.

Thanks so much.

Now to thank the new great team I worked with on this book. Chelsea Barnes, you are amazing, girl. You pulled everything together, managed me and my book, and also provided a super awesome new cover. Without you, I would still be lost. So thank you so very much.

Jennifer Mattison, having you on my editing team rocked. You are quick and efficient. I asked, you answered. It was great to work with you. Thank you so very much.

Candice Barnes, my rocking proofreader! Like your sister, you rock. Thank you so much for being a part of my team.

To all the bloggers out there, thank you for taking the time in sharing my reveals, teasers, and release. Without you, my name would not spread.

And to all indie authors out there. I thank you for giving this girl the courage to do what she always wanted to do. The support I see each and every one of you give each other, it is just amazing. I hope one day I can be part of that special family.

Prologue

Ten years ago…

It was a Friday afternoon when James Samos was called into Connor Green's office. James headed to the office thinking they were going to discuss their weekly run, oblivious of the knowledge Connor held in his hands.

James walked into the dimly lit office, which he had become fairly familiar with over the years. A big mahogany desk and chair sat in the far corner. The black leather furniture had faded, but still remained in the opposite corner. Pictures of sailboats still hung on each wall, and the room smelled of stale smoke as it always had. James walked over and took a seat in the chair offered to him across from his boss.

James looked across the desk at Connor, who wore a grim expression. "Well James, it seems we have a situation."

"A situation?" James swallowed deeply. His heart rate rose. By the look on Connor's face, he knew this wasn't going to be a simple meeting.

"It seems you have taken things that don't belong to you, hmm?" Connor switched on the computer monitor that sat on his desk and turned it in James's direction to show the low-quality video feed of him stealing. Connor let it play a few times to let the reality of the situation sink in.

James's heart stopped for a moment, his breath caught, and then panic set in. Sweat began to develop on the back of his neck, his palms became clammy. He was caught. James thought immediately of his beautiful wife, Amelia, and his sweet daughter, Jenn.

He never thought of them when he was doing dirty deeds. He had kept it all a secret from them. His little girl was friends with Connor's son, Sean. Jenn talked about nothing but the handsome boy who protected her at school. Would Connor really harm his family over this situation?

"You have stolen something of great value from me, and more than once, so I think it is only fair that I steal something of value from you," Connor spat out with full anger behind his words. He pulled a revolver from the top desk drawer and pointed it at James, "Now watch the screen, and see what your actions have cost you."

A few clicks of the mouse and a new video came on, also poor quality. On the screen he saw Amelia, his sweet innocent Amelia. She was searching the living room for something. A sudden noise startled her, so she whipped around to face the door. Someone else appeared in the room, and it wasn't Jenn. A large man dressed in black with a ski mask covering his face appeared in the frame, pointing a gun directly at Amelia. She raised her arms in surrender.

Amelia's mouth moved, but there was no sound. Her body jolted suddenly, not once, but twice. Blood sprayed a short distance from the wounds in her chest. With the video so grainy James was unable to see the life vanish from her beautiful blue eyes, but knew she was gone as she collapsed to the floor.

"No!" James yelled. His only thought now was Jenn as he silently prayed she stayed hidden from the man. Out of the corner of his eye, he noticed her tiny body under a nearby desk, curled up tight. He prayed that neither men noticed her. The screen went black.

Chapter One

Present day…

She was in the void between consciousness and sleep, having just had a routine nightmare. Every damn night it was the same, always the same. Jenn had been having the same dream since she was a child, a beast of a man with dark, beady eyes wearing dark clothing, holding a gun.

Never getting a full picture, or the full scene, only bits and pieces. She could never figure out what they meant. Just as the gun went off, she felt something soft touch her face. She didn't know if it was part of her dream or if it was real. This had never happened in the dream before.

Then she felt it again. No, it definitely wasn't a dream. It was a light touch, a gentle caress of her cheek. Quickly, she made a mental note of her hands and wiggled her fingers and knew that hers were under the blankets. She opened her eyes and met a pair of dark eyes, surrounded by a black mask. The softness she felt on her cheek instantly moved to cover her mouth and nose.

Panic set in, and the fight-or-flight response kicked in. She swiftly pulled her arms from under the blanket to ward off the attack. But attached to the head that held those eyes was a body. A very strong body.

Hovering over her, a pair of strong arms took charge. He grabbed her as she struggled, taking both her wrists in one hand while the other held a cloth on her face.

She fought with all her might. Although she was much smaller than the beast above her, she was never one to give up. As her adrenaline depleted, she became sluggish from the sweet-smelling substance on the cloth, but she tried with all that she had. She managed to slightly shift the position she was in, but it just wasn't enough. She tried kicking her legs, but her strength was waning fast. He was just too big. With her last intake of breath, everything went black.

She woke a short time later, but things didn't feel right. She was in bed, but it wasn't hers. It was hard and lumpy. Something was off. An old musty scent was present. She was used to the vanilla air fresheners in her home. Musty was not vanilla. The room was very quiet. Goose bumps rose on her arms and slowly crept up the back of her neck. Her vision was slightly foggy, and she felt weak. Her legs tingled and she was confused. She couldn't remember what had happened to her. It was as if her mind was playing tricks on her.

Blinking a few times to clear her vision, she realized it was still dark outside. The moon shone dimly through a window, allowing her to make out some of her surroundings. The bed was large, queen-size she thought, and even though it was hard and lumpy, it was still semi-comfortable. Beside the bed was an empty nightstand. Across the room sat a waist-high chest of drawers. She focused on the door momentarily and thought, *Do I test my luck and attempt an escape?*

As she started to get off the bed, her memory began to re-emerge. She remembered leaving the office last evening, same as always. She had made breakfast plans with her father via telephone for the next morning and left to go home. A migraine had put her to bed early, and now she was in this strange place. The memory of a masked man with stormy eyes came to her, a struggle… Shivering, unaware of what was going on, or what was going to happen, she tried to keep from panicking.

Memories flooded her mind of the previous night, like flashing screenshots. As the scenes flew by, she tried to process what little she knew. She sat back on the bed and began to shiver in fear. Who took her? Why did they take her? How was she getting out? All questions, but no answers. The door knob rattled and turned. In walked the man with the mask. He had on a pair of dark-wash jeans and a plain white T-shirt. On his feet were a pair of black Doc Martens. He was carrying a red Solo cup. He turned his eyes in her direction and walked toward her.

"Drink this," a husky voice said from behind the mask. He stared down at her body.

Upon feeling his gaze on her, Jenn realized she was only wearing a skimpy pair of black boxer shorts and a tiny red tank top. Quickly, while trembling, she huddled under the blankets on the bed. Fear radiated from her pores.

He sighed and set the cup on the bedside table. "I am not going to hurt you," he told her. "The water will help flush the chloroform out of your system."

She felt a surge of anger. *Chloroform?* He had already hurt her. The fucking bastard had drugged her. She reacted instinctively, reaching out and slapping the cup. The water, now soaked into the carpet.

"Suit yourself." He growled, shaking his head in frustration. He proceeded to stomp out of the room, shut the door, and lock it.

At least she knew that the door was locked, and she couldn't escape that way. She would have to check for another way out. Maybe the window, but that would have to wait until she stopped shaking.

It seemed like forever before she was finally able to calm down and get her pulse to settle. Jenn got off the bed, tiptoed over to the window, and tried to open it. Of course, it wouldn't budge.

"Damn it," she whispered to herself. She looked out and noticed the bars, knowing then that even if she broke the window, she wasn't getting out that way. Looking around the room, feelings of dread sank in her stomach. She saw no other possible escape routes. She eyed the door again.

She knew the door wouldn't open, but she tried anyway. "Fuck!" She was at a loss, but wasn't ready to give up yet. She wandered back over to the bed and sat down. She put her head in her hands and began to think things through.

Who, what, where, and why? The continuous questions kept circling through her mind. She closed her eyes to think, but all that was present were those eyes, *his* eyes. She needed answers. Puzzles were her thing, but with no clues, there was no way to piece it together. Huffing to herself, still tired and now very frustrated, she decided to curl back up and try to conserve some energy.

She tried to keep the fear at bay, but it continued to overpower her thoughts, keeping her awake. She had never been in a situation like this and it was scary. She could feel dampness on her skin from the sweat she produced, though she was not warm. Even though she had been trying to ignore it, she still trembled a little bit.

With a lack of physical strength, she lay on the bed,

trying to decipher an answer to her problem. There had to be a reason why she was there, locked in a room. Why her quiet little life had been turned upside down.

She laid there until the sun started to shine through the window, and she was able to make out more of her surroundings. The morning light made the room look less like a dungeon. Her blankets were a soft pale pink, and the walls were a creamy white. The curtains were made of simple white lace, and the nightstand and dresser were a matching set of what appeared to be white oak. The floor was covered in a soft gray carpet, and she noticed a light switch by the door. There were no pictures of any sort or clues of any kind to help her figure out who had taken her captive.

Feeling a little braver and sure of herself, she approached the door and banged on it. "Let me out of here, you bastard!" she yelled. All she got in return was silence. She pounded again and again, but nothing.

So she just yelled. "Ahhhh!" Frustrated and scared, reacting without thinking, she kicked the door and whimpered in pain. She hadn't meant to kick so hard since she wasn't wearing any shoes. She looked around the room once more in search of something to throw, but she knew there was nothing. She hobbled back to the bed and began to cry. "Why is this happening? Why me? I haven't done anything." She continued to ramble on and on and didn't realize the man had returned to the room and was standing in the doorway watching her.

"You done yet?" he asked her offensively. Startled, she quickly shifted her body into a defensive huddle on the bed. He stood there staring at her, never moving from the doorway. He still wore that damn ski mask. She wanted nothing more than to rip it off him.

She wanted to know who this man was, wanted to see his face. She wanted to piece the whole puzzle together. His nose, his jaw, everything. Match up the rest of the face with those eyes. Figure out the man behind the mask. She would have to wait it out for the perfect opportunity.

Choking back tears, she asked, "Why am I here?" She wanted answers. "Who are you?"

"Demanding little thing, aren't you?" he responded. He shifted his stance, scratched his chin, and then shoved his hands in his jean pockets. Never giving up eye contact.

"Please…" she begged. She trembled and peeked up at him, trying her best to look innocent and sweet.

He shook his head. "Now, Jenn, if I were able to give you all the answers, we wouldn't be in this mess, now would we?"

She needed to get answers from him. He seemed to know who she was; she didn't know how, but she wouldn't be giving up. By the way he spoke, it seemed like a game to him, and she really didn't want to play. "Can you tell me anything?" she pleaded, in a sweet tone. She tried to act innocent, that particular tone having worked to her advantage with men before. But, it wasn't helping now.

"In due time, little one," he returned softly. "In that time, you will need to behave, listen to everything I say, and follow any orders I give to you. That is, if you want to survive this."

Jenn's mind went on full alert. If she wanted to survive this? Her body jerked back, her chest ached, and the sobbing started again. "What do I need to do? I don't want to die."

Okay, she had done it. She was beginning to cave. Like a damsel in distress, looking for her knight in shining armor, she was ready to beg. Tears streaking down her cheeks, she bit her lip, waiting for an answer.

He shifted on his feet again and took a deep breath. Was he going to tell her something? Should she get her hopes up?

"For now, rest. Think of your past, your childhood. Does anything stick out that would trigger any thought of why anyone would want to hurt you? Or want you laid out on a concrete slab, dead? When I return, we'll talk more." Standing straight up, he turned to leave, but looked back over his shoulder just before he did. "Also keep in mind, if you don't listen or follow my orders, punishment is non-negotiable." Then he walked out, shutting the door and locking it once again.

Chapter Two

Sean leaned against the wall just outside the room, head in his hands. He was frustrated about the whole situation. The questions she kept asking, the memories all just sitting right there. His job sucked.

Just thinking about it, he couldn't believe he was following his father's orders again. He didn't know how much more he could take. Would he ever get out of his father's grasp and live his own life? But the right question was—would his father let him live?

His father had killed for lesser things. Sean should know. He had killed a man for him. That blood was on his hands. He's hated every minute of his tasks, but he'd taken the abuse for so long. He tried to get away a few times, but his father sent his brothers, Jake and Dominic, after him every time. They would belittle him, abuse him, and give him all of the grunt work, making him know his place.

While training to be an assassin, a drug smuggler, and more, he'd lost all aspects of control in his life. He needed to get his life back, not just for him, but for his sanity. He wasn't a little kid anymore. He was a man, and a man lived his own life, right?

As soon as he'd been old enough, control was removed from his life, and the beatings were constant reminders of who was. He had become so weak when it came to his father, and now after taking this job, he felt trapped. He had hoped that his father's anger would never reach her. But it was too late.

He was kicking himself for taking the job, for opening that file folder and agreeing to kidnap Jenn, his Jenn. He wasn't sure how long he would be able to play his part in his father's twisted game. He was thankful for the mask he wore, even though deep down he thought she would still recognize him. Jenn and he went way back, they had a history. To him, she was precious, always had been and always would be.

Hurting her was the last thing he ever wanted to do. His father's game was all for revenge.

It was always a live-or-die situation when it came to his father. Didn't matter if you were his wife, son, or even his own mother, when shit hit the fan, the bodies piled up.

It had been three years since he last saw her face-to-face, and oh how he had missed her. He missed her smile, her laugh, and everything else about her. A full three years since he felt the life he was living was too dangerous for her to be around. He didn't want to put her in harm's way any more than he had already had. His father's business was getting riskier by the day.

He'd watched her from a distance, hoping the past would never catch up to her. Even over the span of time, he couldn't get her out of his mind, no matter how hard he tried. She had always been his little secret. The one he'd hidden from his father. His decision to let her go was the safe one, or so he thought.

Jenn hadn't changed much over the years, but she had matured beautifully. Full perky breasts laid under her tiny tank top. Her hips begged to be held, and that gorgeous hair of hers had lengthened. The tight curls she wore as a child had softened into large winding locks down her back. Her eyes were brighter than he remembered. Bluer than any ocean, and they carried a secret.

It was that secret that brought her into the sick game his father had laid out for her. He only hoped he could keep his older brothers away from her. This was his mark. He took this job because he didn't want to see any harm come to her. He hoped he could carry through with his plan. Dying wasn't a welcomed option, but he wasn't going to watch Jenn die either. The whole situation was a clusterfuck.

Sean's family had power and money. They never had that when he was younger, but his father made sure to exploit it as he grew older. Drugs and guns were his father's business. He didn't want a part in it, but his father never gave him the option. Since his older brothers were already taking part in the trade, dear old dad felt that he should make it a family business. The day Sean agreed to join, not by choice, was the day he regretted most. Being beaten into submission, he was told his life was his father's life. He was forced by gunpoint to murder his first victim. Yes, he was filled with regret. Sean regretted not saying fuck you to his father and having them put a bullet in him. But he didn't. And since that day, his father had controlled every possible aspect of Sean's life.

Every woman Sean brought home, whether it was a simple fuck or even just a basic friend, his father chased off at some point. He said they were never good enough. Accused them of being snitches, saying he couldn't trust them around the business. Sean had become so frustrated with his life that he took to the gym and worked out his frustrations.

Sean was not a scrawny kid anymore - He was a tall, well-chiseled man now, and had even gone as far as getting tattoos and a nipple ring. He now had pecs women swooned over, and arms were so well formed that his shirts were tight around them. His thigh muscles were well defined. He was proud of what he had transformed his body into. It may have taken some time, but it wasn't like he didn't have it. He even got laser-eye surgery to get rid of his glasses. It was one thing his father didn't control—his body, his looks, with the exception of a bruise every now and then.

Sean pulled the mask off his face. Desperate for a drink, he pushed himself away from the wall and walked down the hall to the living room. He had his orders, now to figure out what was next. Everything was laid out, plain and simple. He read the file, knew the job, and fucking hated it. Once he took in Jenn's weeping form, and knowing what was in store for her, he wasn't sure he'd be able to follow through with that plan. He needed to figure something out, and fast.

He told his father he could do the job, that he wouldn't betray him. He got a beating as a warning. His father knew that he and Jenn had a past from attending the same schools, but he never knew how close they truly were.

When his father said either do the job right or he was sending one of Sean's brothers, he knew he had to do it. If one of his brothers were to complete this job, who knew what would happen to her. His brothers were complete narcissistic bastards. But for now, he had a part to play. Until the time came that he had a choice in the matter, he'd play the part to the best of his ability in front of her, and especially when his father and brothers were watching..

Chapter Three

Punishment, she thought. What kind of goddamned punishment was he talking about? What kind of trouble was she in? Shivers ran up her spine. After the man left the room, Jenn had nothing but time; she had nowhere she could go, no place to hide. So she laid on the bed, curled up with the pillow, and prayed for answers.

Someone wanted her dead? Lying on a concrete slab in the morgue? She shuddered with the thought. Who the heck would want her dead? She was a lonely receptionist at an insurance office with no special skills. She knew how to file, answer phones, and do data entry. Nothing exceptional there.

She grew up in the town she worked in, and she had never been in trouble with anyone. No speeding tickets, no parking tickets. She had never wronged any man she dated that she could remember. Not that she actually dated much. She had never backstabbed any of her friends, not that she really had many of them either. She kept to herself most days. She was a shy, quiet woman, always had been. She was not a recluse or a hermit, but wasn't one to overly socialize with anyone.

She had gotten picked on when she was younger and

all through her teens. She had never been able to break through that puny picket fence of shelter and grow a backbone strong enough to stand up for herself. Little by little, she was trying. Now would be the time that she could do it. Well, she hoped.

Nothing in her past helped to explain her kidnapping. She'd been a good girl her whole life. She didn't have sex until she was twenty. She never felt comfortable enough with her body to do something so intimate. And when she finally did feel good enough to do such a thing, that relationship didn't last. The guy turned out to be a jackass. But she did get a gorgeous necklace from him, so that was a plus. There was only one other guy that had been in her life and that was Sean, her best friend. He had always been there for her. Until one day, he just wasn't. Things changed so fast in that time. It had been just over three years ago. She thought they were going to be more than friends, well she really hoped. Things were leading up to it. She felt the chemistry between them, but then he just disappeared. Out to dinner and gone, no word since. Did this have anything to do with that? Her mind was running a mile a minute.

Wringing her fingers tight, she glanced around the room, wishing something would jump out to her to give her answers. Nothing did. She squeezed her eyes shut, and all she could see were those eyes. Mysterious, gray eyes peering at her, through her, like they knew her but they didn't, did they? She could get lost in the depth of those eyes. They were dreamy eyes, but also vaguely familiar. She just couldn't pick it out.

He told her she had to try and remember, but remember what? She tried to reach as far back in her memory as she could. Everything that might jump out at her to be a cause for this situation, was a dead end. She was a good kid, never got in trouble, no record, no problem with the police. The same thoughts tumbled through her mind over and over until she drew a blank.

She winced as the aura of a migraine hit. Her peripheral vision became blurred with twinkled stars, and nausea struck just like when she ate something wrong. The pain began in her forehead with a nagging stab, as if a screwdriver was slowly being driven through her skull. She took a deep breath and hoped it would not go full blown. At the moment, it was tolerable.

She had been getting migraines for years. With being abducted without her medication, she was going to have to suffer through it. And on top of it all, she had to pee. If only she was at home, she would be taking an Axert, a fast-acting migraine medication, and some Gravol. She could ease the pain with a cup of peppermint tea and nap on her soft bed with an ice pack on her neck.

Jenn eased up from the bed and slowly moved to the door. She knocked on it. If she pounded, she knew she'd regret it with her throbbing head as bad as it was already.

"I need to go the bathroom. Please…" She spoke as loud as she could tolerate. She leaned against the door. After a minute or two she heard footsteps. She stepped back and waited.

The door opened and there he stood, mask and all. "You need something?" he asked her with curiosity.

"I need the bathroom, please," she whispered.

"I'll take you, but only if you promise not to run." He eyed her, opening the door further. "If you run, I will catch you."

She looked him right in the eye and promised, "I will not run, I swear it." But she was not sure if she was going to keep her word. Even though she was in too much pain to do anything except curl up and cry, she felt she needed to at least try to get away. She just needed to plan it for the right time. If the opportunity arose, she was taking it.

He escorted her by her arm and lower back, down two doors to a quaint little bathroom. It was small, but clean, with creamy beige walls and a small, round mirror hanging on the wall above an oval sink that sat in a beautiful mahogany vanity with a white marble countertop. Next to the designer tub was a basic toilet. Between the toilet and tub was a small window with a simple white curtain, but there was no way a body could fit through that window, bars and all.

She stepped into the room. He followed right behind her, so she stopped. "Can a girl get some privacy, please?" She breathed, afraid of what he may say. She looked back at him and hoped he would at least give her that little bit of dignity.

Glancing up and down her body, he smirked. "Don't do anything that you will regret, hmm?" He turned and quietly shut the door behind him.

She knew he wouldn't go far. She knew he didn't trust her. He was probably just outside the door, so she had to be quick and quiet. While she emptied her bladder in the porcelain toilet, she darted her eyes around the room for objects she could use for her defense. She saw a hairbrush, toothbrush, and toothpaste on the vanity. She quietly moved the shower curtain aside and noticed a bar of soap and shampoo, but nothing that could help her. She finished and washed her hands. Once she was sorted, she opened the door. He was casually leaning against the wall opposite the bathroom, legs crossed at the ankles, his hands sitting at the side of his body, just waiting. He was sporting an amused expression through the mask, which she only noticed because of the tiny crinkles he had at the corners of his eyes. He wasn't even trying to hide his smirk. Even his eyes were full of amusement, and she had no idea why. She stepped forward, and he stepped away from the wall, moved toward her, and proceeded to guide her back to the room.

He placed his hand on the small of her back while walking.

"Don't touch me," she said through gritted teeth.

He removed his hand with no complaint.

Now was the time, she thought. She took a deep breath when she felt he was close enough and rammed her elbow into his gut. Hard. She didn't think twice, she didn't even look back at him to see if she caused any damage or not, she just began to run.

"Hmph," he grunted out from the contact. He reached out for her, but missed. He sprinted after her. "Fuck!" he growled.

She didn't get far before she was knocked down to the floor with a thump. Instantly, he was on top of her, growling like a ravenous animal, and she was his trapped prey.

He eased up from his position and flipped her onto her back. He braced her arms hard with his hands and leaned into her face while breathing hard. "You said you wouldn't run."

She tried struggling, all fear aside. She managed to buck her hips, but it was not enough to get anywhere. Frustrated and breathing deep, she gave up. "You can't blame a girl for trying." She gave a fast look over his torso. The way his tee shirt strained tight over his muscular chest and arms. She thought she felt something when she bucked against him, but couldn't confirm visually. Her eyes lazily moved up to his, and she smirked at him. So he likes to play rough does he? Maybe this will be the way to gain a distraction for an escape strategy. She supposed she could try to play his games. She'd need to shove her fear aside. She just needed to figure out how. But first she needed to get rid of this damn frigging migraine.

He sighed deeply and eased up off her body, pulling her up by her arms. "Just get in the room, woman!" he ordered grumpily.

She winced at his loud voice.

"What are you whining about?" he barked.

Instantly, her hands went to her head, tears brimming in her eyes.

Shaking his head. "You have a migraine, don't you?" He spoke softly.

Her head snapped toward him and that was a mistake, if she ever knew one. "What would you know about migraines?" she spat out, and tears started to free fall involuntarily down her cheeks. She rushed over to the bed and curled up into a ball like a fetus in the womb.

"I know a lot about you, Jenn." He spoke calmly to her. "If you only knew," he mumbled, but she didn't understand him.

"Leave me alone." She sobbed, rubbing her temples, and wished the pain would go away. Wishing the whole nightmare would just end.

She didn't hear him leave the room. The only sound she heard was the thumping in her temples. The next thing she heard was something being set down on the nightstand beside her. She opened her eyes to see what it was. The man had brought in a glass of water and beside it laid two tiny pills. They looked like Advil, but she wasn't sure. She glanced up, and he was standing beside her. She jumped a little. She hadn't noticed him. He was so quiet, so still. "Take those. They will help with the pain," he whispered to her, watching closely.

"How do I know you're not just trying to drug me?" She looked him right in the eye. His eyes twinkled with mischief. Like he knew something, but was never going to tell her. She was not backing down from him. Her life depended on it. Her survival instincts kicked in, but she still had to be cautious. That fence was coming down in pieces.

"You don't. But like I told you already, you need to follow my orders or suffer the consequences." He leaned down until they were face-to-face. His eyes bored into hers. "You want the pain gone, you take the pills. You don't want it gone, then go ahead and suffer. That choice I will give you, but it will be one of the few you will get from this day forward." He stood, crossed his arms across his chest, and stood there.

She was at the breaking point with the pain in her head. She wanted it gone. She couldn't think straight, and her peripheral vision was blurry. She needed it to end, so she did the one thing she never thought she would, she trusted him. Just this once. She took the pills. She also drank all the water and prayed that the water was clean. "Thank you," she muttered and laid back on the bed. If the man was not lying to her, then in about an hour the horrible pain should start to subside. Maybe by showing the man that little bit of trust she would be able to get an answer or two from him. Well, she could hope, couldn't she?

Chapter Four

Sean was pleased that she took the pills. It proved that she was not naïve or careless, and she just might submit to him in all that he had to put her through. "You're welcome." He backed away from the bed, turned, and began to leave the room.

"Please don't leave" she begged and bowed her head, "I don't understand why I am here, and you have shown this little piece of kindness. Can't you tell me anything? Just give me a tiny hint?" she said, looking up at him with pleading eyes.

"Babe, I mean, Jenn." Fuck, he thought to himself. She needed to stop talking. He couldn't slip up like that; she'd figure him out. "If I were able, I would tell you. But this is not my game being played. I'm not permitted to tell you the rules," he told her and left the room once again.

Sean was seriously starting to struggle with everything he had done over the years. With his demons, his wrong choices. He really wanted to tell Jenn everything. His deep feelings for her were starting to surface, and she only asked for a hint, so what could it hurt? Well, it could hurt him if his father found out. He had already gotten a warning hadn't he? But how would he find out? He had to shake that thought.

Down the hall, he heard the phone ring. He took his mask off and went to answer it.

"Hello."

"Do you have her?" the voice asked. He could never forget that voice, no matter how hard he tried. He'd heard that voice his entire life. Very seldom was it a happy voice. He hated it.

"Yes, Dad, I do." He spoke with a flat tone.

"Can you handle this? I don't want your prissy emotions getting in the way with this job," he hissed out.

"I got it, Dad. I got it," he huffed back. "When do you want her?" He was struggling. He hated talking to his dad, but seeing him was worse.

"I am sending your brother, Jake, over there. I need you to go to her place and pick some things up. I have a list of what you need."

"Why can't Jake go get the shit?" Knowing that his father was up to no good, he had to at least ask.

"This is your job. Don't fuck it up." It was not a request, it was an order. That meant he had to face his father sooner rather than later. The last time he saw him was when he got his warning.

He remembered going to his father's home, entering his den. He saw his father's smug face and felt all the hate filling the room. His father had tossed a folder at him, and his fate was signed right then. If he could go back and do things differently, he would. When his father took his fists to him as usual, he made his point clear, and now here he was.

He didn't want to leave her here with his brother, but he had to trust that nothing would happen while he was gone. What the hell was he talking about, trust his brother, yeah right. But what choice did he have?

"All right, send him. When he gets here, I will be on my way."

As usual, his brothers knew things long before he did. Just as he hung up the phone with his father, Jake waltzed into the house. Now he had to play nice with his fucking brother, oh joy. He gritted his teeth.

"Hey, Sean." Jake nodded at him. "So, how's the chick?" Of course Jake would refer to Jenn as a chick; all women were chicks to him. Jake was a ladies' man when he was on the prowl. Standing six foot four, and built like a UFC fighter, Jake could attract any woman he wanted, and he took what he wanted, too. The women loved him. He prayed Jenn would be safe with him, and Jake stayed out of her room. He really hoped nothing happened while he was gone. He prayed that his brother had some shred of the man he once knew inside of him.

"She is fine. Just leave her alone," he grunted out. Shit, Sean shouldn't have said that. Jake may think something was amiss with the situation. Best better cover his butt now, so shit didn't hit the fan. "She's sleeping, should stay that way until I get back. I won't be long." He tried to give warning, but that never usually worked with his brothers. He could never forget the night Jake overstepped Sean's directions during a job. A thug was shot, drugs went missing, causing the outcome to not work out in his favor. His father kicked the shit out of him for it, and his brother just walked away as if nothing happened. He knew he couldn't trust Jake, but he had to hope. No. He could beg the lords above that he wouldn't do anything stupid to screw this up. Sean got his shoes and jacket on and left to head to his father's home.

After a twenty-minute drive, Sean pulled his '69

Camaro up to the front of the large ranch-style home that his father currently lived in. It was nothing like the home the family grew up in. This one was newer, more modern, compared to the old-fashioned plantation-style home he had loved and grown up in. It wasn't until his father felt he needed a smaller home that he bought the ranch. The rest of the family had already moved out, no need for all the extra space. Sean got out, rounded the car, stepped up the three stairs to the door, and entered. "Dad!" he yelled. "Where you at, old man?" He knew he wouldn't leave without getting hit at least once, so why not throw one jab at his father.

While walking through the small, bright main entrance that contained a large wooden coat rack against one wall and a tiny key rack that contained two sets of keys on the opposite wall, he heard his father bellow, "In the den, Sean."

Time to put his game face on. Sean knew his father could read him like a book, so one wrong look or wrong answer and there would be hell to pay. Especially after the 'old man' jab. After a few deep breaths, he trudged toward the den. He was nervous; he knew what his father could do to him.

His father hung up the phone, grumbling. "Stupid detectives won't leave me alone. Always harassing me about my business. Trying to nab me on something." He started right in on Sean. While sitting forward in his chair, a dark glare in his eyes and sneer on his face, he simply spoke. "Did you tell her anything?"

"No." Why couldn't his father just trust him? He was never the one to screw him over at any job. It was always his brothers, but he was always the one to get the blame. Was his father that hateful toward him?

His father observed him, his gaze hard enough that it was like he was looking right through him. He looked angry, like he was ready to pounce. "You are lying to me," he spat.

Sean knew this was coming. His father had major trust issues since some employees started stealing from him. Even though he was family, he still didn't trust him. The trust issues had built over the years. His father stood from his chair and came toward him. Fists clenched, a sneer on his face.

"I am not lying. I told her nothing," Sean told him as calmly as he could. His muscles became tense, the hair on the back of his neck stood on end. The fear of his father was beginning to rise. He knew what was coming, and as usual, it did. His father took his swing and made first contact. A right hook, square to Sean's jaw. It nearly knocked him down. But Sean kept himself steady. He could taste the coppery-like flavor; he didn't dare spit the blood out. Never would he give his father the satisfaction. He was not going to give him another reason to smack him around. He wiped his mouth with the back of his hand. "Dad, I didn't tell her anything!" he gritted between his still blood-soaked teeth. He was trying to contain his own anger.

"Well, you fucking better not, if you know what's best for you." His father turned and returned to his chair. He reached over to a small table and grabbed a small piece of paper and handed it to Sean. "Go to her place and retrieve these items. They should hold her over until I need her," he ordered. "Now get out of my face. I have other business to tend to."

Sean clenched his fists and swiftly left the room and the house. He spat out the blood that was pooling in his mouth on the driveway and took a few deep breathes. He got in his car and sped away. Relief set in once he was out of the house, away from his father. He hated being held responsible for shit he didn't do, but running away was so hard. Maybe it was time. Every job he did for him was getting harder and harder to do. It was like his father had a hate-on for him and was trying to push his limits. With those limits met, it was time to make a plan.

Chapter Five

Jenn heard a phone ring somewhere. That meant there was a form of communication in the house. Until she could figure out a way to get to the phone, she supposed she should just lay back and let the pain medication kick in. Then she could try to figure things out.

She managed to relax enough to fall asleep. She was just starting to dream about those mysterious, but familiar, sexy gray eyes when suddenly the door to the room was thrown open and startled her awake. She shot up in the bed and looked over. A man stood there. He wasn't the same man from earlier. This guy was bigger, taller and he didn't have a mask on. He was built, broad and thick. He looked like a fighter. He reminded her of the sexy, UFC fighter, George St-Pierre, one good-looking fighter. He had on a pair of tight black jeans and a white muscle shirt. His hair was dark brown, styled in a sort of a buzz cut. He had a set of deep gray eyes, and he was grinning at her. The grin was evil-looking, like he had something on his mind, and she really did not like it. His nose was sharp and slightly crooked, as if it had been broken once or twice. He had a well-chiseled jaw covered with a five-o'clock shadow, and he was sporting a single diamond stud in his left ear.

"Well, well, well, what do we have here?" spoke the brute man, sending chills through her. "Looks like we have a sweet piece of ass, sitting all alone on the big ol' bed here." The man winked at her.

She shivered from the fear starting to rise from deep inside. "What do you want?" she whispered, gripping the blanket tight to her chest. A sudden sweat broke out on the back of her neck, and her pulse began to accelerate.

The man closed the door and sauntered over to the bed. "Don't worry, little thing. I won't do anything you won't like." He smirked and sat on the edge of the bed.

Jenn pushed her body as far back on the bed as it would allow her. She did not want him to touch her. He was good-looking, in a scary kind of way, but the way he was leering at her didn't sit right with her. He stared at her like a ravenous lion, and she was a piece of raw meat. She was not prepared to be his meal. "Please, don't touch me," she pleaded innocently. Shivers ran through her. She wasn't sure if she had the strength to fight, but she sure would do her best to try.

The man who was making her feel more scared by the minute smiled at her and reached toward her leg. "Come on now, sugar. Big daddy isn't going to hurt you." He smirked. "Unless you ask him to." He leaned further into her and grabbed her ankle. "We're just going to talk." He winked.

She kicked her leg at him.

He laughed. He reached and grabbed again, strengthening his grip.

"Let go of me, you big ape!" She cried out and tried to kick him away again.

Her struggle only seemed to urge him on, as he moved closer and reached with his other hand. He grabbed her other ankle and pulled her down the bed, removing the blankets covering her in the process.

She screamed and started to fight him.

Again her thoughts ran frantically: How was she going to get out of this? Was he going to hurt her? Was he going to rape her? Was he going to kill her? He was too big to fight and screaming just urged him on. Fuck! The day couldn't get any worse. She continued to struggle, kicking her legs. The man laughed as if he enjoyed the fight. She started to swing her arms, anything to get her out of the position she was in. Luck decided to be on her side, and she could hardly believe it. One of her swings actually made contact. She hit him in the side of his face, and pretty hard. Hard enough that it hurt her hand.

"You stupid bitch!" he growled and released her ankles. He full-out smacked her across her face.

Damn, that hurt.

He pinned her by her arms and used his body to hold the rest of her down. "You hit me, bitch," he spat out.

The man did not look that sexy when he was mad, she thought. She could feel the blood drain from her nose, and her lip was starting to throb. He had hit her good. She had never been hit before. She didn't like the feeling at all. "I'm sorry." She covered her face and turned it to the side with the hope he wouldn't hit her again. Her body shook once again, her nerves in overdrive of the unknown. "You were scaring me. I wasn't thinking." She grabbed at straws, anything to get the man to back off. Her eyes filled with tears, but she tried to hold them back.

"You fucking better be, bitch." He sat back on his heels with a grin. "So, where were we?" His hand grazed her upper arm and then down her abdomen to her thigh.

She cringed, and he laughed.

"Get off of me, you asshole," she yelled, unaware of how it slipped out. It was like she had Tourette's and super mood swings all at once, but she knew it felt good to say. Though angry and scared, she was gaining some strength to fight back, and it took everything in her not to spit at him. She really needed to get her shit together.

"A feisty one, eh?" The asshole of a man laughed out and continued on his excursion of touching her body. He cupped her breasts in his hands. "Oh, I like these." His eyes had an evil glint.

She didn't like his touch. She needed him to stop. "Fuck off!" she swore, and in a flash she swung her fist again, and luck was still with her. Contact again.

"Fuck!" he yelled, and in quick response punched her back. He grabbed at her shirt, and he began to tear it off her.

Adrenaline surged and even with tears running down her face, Jenn fought with everything she had. She managed to get her leg in the position to her advantage and nailed him in the balls.

He screamed and grabbed his crotch. "Bitch!" he yelled and crawled off her and the bed.

She tucked herself up in a defensive position, shaking slightly with tears on her face. She wasn't letting him get to her again.

"Ah, fuck woman! Tears? You think that shit works on me?" He shook his head, adjusted his balls, and began to walk away. "Fucking women! Nothing like busting the mood. Literally! You ain't worth it, bitch," he mumbled. Then he walked out the door and shut and locked it.

It was getting dark outside by the time Jenn was able to stop crying. Almost an entire day had gone by, and she had not eaten a single morsel of food. The only water she had was with the pills. Why would he starve her when he was nice enough to give her medication for her migraine? Where was he, and who was that other man? Why was he so much scarier than the man in the mask? She felt weak from the lack of food and was sore from the abuse she took. She wasn't sure how much more she could handle before she completely unraveled. She was going to have to dig deep within herself and break down those walls that protected her, and fight for her life. She was not ready to die, not today, not tomorrow, not anytime soon.

Chapter Six

Sean arrived at her moderate-sized, two-bedroom house and entered the front door with the key he had on his key chain - The key he took from her key chain. He wasn't going to break in this time when there was no need. He took his time to look around. Taking in every smell in each room. Natural or flower scented, he accepted it all.

With the sunlight shining in her sheer-draped windows, he was able to take it all in. He noticed the black leather furniture organized just so in the living room. The oak coffee table and end tables with doilies on top, which made him smile. Always the girlie girl she was, he thought. A large flat-screen TV hung on the wall, and shelves full of pictures and knickknacks were scattered about.

Just left of the very large open living room was a door leading to a bedroom, and off to the right was a door to a fairly spacious modern bathroom. Her kitchen was big with an island separating it from the living room. The color scheme of the home was of bold dark colors, and the floors were all hardwood. As he searched her place, he found photos of family, and it made him think of the days of their childhood together. The good and the bad. It also made him remember the day he told her he just wasn't good enough for her. He could see the love in her eyes that day.

It was a typical Saturday for them. They had made plans to hang out and go to the movies that night. It was actually preplanned. Routine for them, been doing it since we were the ripe age of fourteen. Friends till the end, they promised each other. But one of his father's jobs that he did that day set him on an emotional roller coaster. It had him changing his mindset, and he knew he had to push Jenn away. He didn't want her in the crossfire, didn't want her getting hurt. That day, Sean had made his first kill.

With what was still blood on his hands, he met up with Jenn at a coffee shop to break the news. She was her chipper self. Full of smiles and love in her eyes. They ordered their coffee and sat in silence for a few moments.

Jenn couldn't contain herself in the silence. "So what was so important that we are here now, Sean?" She smiled big at him. It hurt him to see that smile, knowing what he was about to do.

He reached across the table and grasped her hand. "Babe, there are things happening, feelings are changing. I can see it. I can feel it." He squeezed her hand and took a deep breath. "I want you to know I love you, babe, but I'm no good for you. I have done things over the years as we've grown together from friends to… whatever this is, and…" He looked deep into her eyes and waited with bated breath. "We are not little kids anymore."

Her eyes watered. "What do you mean, Sean?" She pulled her hand free from his and wiped her eye. "I thought things…" She began to mumble. "I mean I thought…" She couldn't finish, she was so confused and upset.

"Babe."

"Don't babe me, you jerk."

He sighed. "Jenn, you don't understand." He slumped back in his seat. "Shit is happening, and you just, you just… I don't want you to get hurt." He crossed his arms across his chest. He was getting frustrated. He hated having to do this. He truly did love her, but he needed to get away from her, for her safety. He didn't want her to know what he was doing, what he had done. She would hate him, just like he hated himself.

"Hurt? The only person hurting me is you, Sean." She reached for her purse and pulled out a Kleenex. "I don't understand. I love…"

Sean couldn't hear her say it, he knew he would buckle. He had to get out of there so when she started to say those words, he got up and ran out.

There were photos of her and her father, old and new. Some with her and her mother when she was a child. No recent ones with her mother since she passed away when Jenn was just thirteen. A robbery gone wrong, they said. Sean knew that was just a cover story. Her father didn't want Jenn knowing what kind of side business he was running. The kind of business that had gotten him in deep shit and ended up causing the death of his wife.

Sean's father and Jenn's father had become rivals while the pair of them were in school together. He learned all about it as he got older. The fight for territory for buying and selling their merchandise was a blind spot to Jenn, but it was not so much for Sean. Having older brothers that partook in the business brought Sean into the loop. Once Sean got involved, he did everything he could to prevent Jenn from knowing about it. And to do so, as time went, he withdrew himself from her life, little by little with hopes that she would not notice what was happening right in her own neighborhood. With the exception of hanging with her on their preplanned nights, Sean began to distance himself.

He found a black knapsack in her closet, like one she may have used for yoga, and started to load the bag with the listed items as he found them. The list consisted of personal items like clothing, undergarments, running shoes, personal hygiene products, and lastly a locket. It was described as having a thin silver chain with a heart-shaped silver decal pendant on the end, which framed a blazing blue diamond. He went over to her dresser and on top sat a black marble jewelry box. He opened the box and sitting right inside was the locket. He grabbed it and left the room. Once he packed everything in the bag, an idea occurred to him. He thought that if he wasn't allowed to mention anything to her, maybe a visual hint would suffice to get her mind moving. When Sean was looking over the photos on her mantle beside the TV, he noticed an old photo that shocked him. It was a picture of him, Jenn, and her mother about a week before her mother passed. He remembered that unforgettable day well. It was the first day of spring, and they had their first barbecue of the season. They had flown kites and rode bikes together while Jenn's parents watched over them. It was also the day he finally realized he was in love with Jenn. He never told her, she was still too young, as was he. Sean was not ready to ruin the friendship they had at a young age. Grabbing the photo and jamming it into the bag, he let himself out of the house, locking it up tight.

Sean returned to his home later than he expected. Jake was sitting on the couch drinking a beer. Once Jake noticed him, he chugged the beer down and got up, jacket in hand. Jake kept his head down as he walked out.

"See ya, Jake," Sean yelled after him. That was strange, he thought. Usually Jake was more talkative. Sean set the bag down by the hallway and went to retrieve a beer for himself. He needed to calm his nerves before he went in to see Jenn.

Chapter Seven

Two beers and a roast beef sandwich later, Sean was feeling much calmer and ready to deal with Jenn. Putting on his mask, he grabbed the bag and walked down to her room. He stood there for a moment, listening - It was too quiet; maybe she was sleeping. He unlocked the door, opened it, and started to walk in. The room was dark, but he could make out the lump on the bed. Jenn was curled up under the blankets. He could hear her soft breaths coming in and out slowly. He quietly advanced farther into the room with the bag and started to put the items in place. He put the clothing in the dresser drawers and set the photograph on the nightstand along with the locket. He glanced down at what should have been her beautiful face and gasped. She was sporting a blackened eye, had dry blood around her nose, and her lip was split. Shit, what the hell!

Jenn seemed to wake when he got closer to the bed. She peeked up at him and started yelling, "Please, no more." Then she tried to cover her face with her hands.

"Oh, Christ, Jenn, I am not going to hurt you. Shit!" Sean reached out to touch her, but saw her flinch so he backed off. "Did the other man do this? Please, tell me what happened." He tried to plead with his eyes. He had never seen her hurt like this before, not once in all the years he had known her. Seeing the injuries made him ache inside.

"He... he..." she stuttered. After taking a few breaths, she spoke again. "He touched me, he grabbed me, and..." The tears started to run down her cheeks. "He pulled me down on the bed." She sobbed louder. "I tried to fight him, and I hit him. He got mad."

"For fuck's sake, he was told to leave you alone, goddamn it!" Sean was pissed. He stood and started to pace the room. Clenching his fists, gritting his teeth, angry that he trusted Jake with her. What the hell was he even thinking? He knew Jake was a total prick and rough with the ladies. Why couldn't his brother listen to him for at least once in his fucked-up life.

He didn't know how he could let his father even consider causing any harm to sweet, innocent Jenn. To allow him to use her as a pawn, a toy. He began to internally fight with himself. He needed to fix this right away. "Jenn." He looked into her eyes, pleading with her. He reached over to the photo and grabbed it. He handed it to her and watched for her reaction. "Here, I brought this from your house. It looked like a special picture, so I thought you'd like it."

"You were in my home again?" she screeched out, then looked down at the picture and seemed to go into a daze.

As he watched her eyes flicker from person to person in the frame, the emotions spread across her face. An ache formed in his chest.

"Want to talk about it?" Sean probed. Getting her to talk was something he remembered being good at years ago. He needed to grab for at least one memory so he could empathize, attempt to earn some trust from her.

She seemed to be debating among her thoughts.

Trying to decide whether to talk or not, he wasn't sure. He heard a little sigh come from her.

"Well the little girl is me, of course, and that beautiful woman there is my mom. She's no longer with us, and the devilishly handsome young man was my savior, Sean. He was my world, my rock. He disappeared once we got older, and I miss him very much." She looked up from the photo to him with tears in her eyes.

Sean's heart sank. He didn't realize how much hurt he had caused her when he distanced himself from her. Back then, he had known it was for the best. The look of sadness in her eyes now, he knew he was going to be a dead man. He couldn't do this job as his father wanted anymore. He couldn't do this job, any job, period. "Jenn, I'm sorry you are hurting. I am very sorry that that man hurt you. I'm sorry that your mother is gone. I am also very, very sorry that your friend has not been there for you, protecting you from what you are going through now." He wasn't sure if he just wrote his own death certificate, or if Jenn would understand, or if she would even let him explain after he did what he was struggling to do next. Or if she would just flat-out hate him.

"You don't know about my life, the hurts, or the pain I have been through. What exactly are you apologizing for? For taking me unwillingly from my home? Drugging me and holding me captive in this room? You personally have not physically hurt me, so which are you sorry for?" She looked down at the picture once again.

He watched her tracing her fingers over the faces, stopping on his.

"Sean?" she mumbled.

He watched her gracefully handle the photo and a tear ran down her cheek. She had mumbled his name. Has she figured him out yet? Is now the time to reveal himself and beg for forgiveness? Could he save them both from the massive mess they were going to be in? "Jenn," he questioned, "have you figured out why you are here yet?" He backed away to give her space. If she was going to flip out, he did not want to be in the range of emotional, swinging arms.

She looked up at him with what looked like recognition. "Would it have anything to do with my mother's death?" She appeared calm, sitting up in the bed facing him.

He was surprised she was so calm. He figured she would have reacted differently. "Partly," he told her, "but there's more." He had to be honest. He couldn't let it go on anymore. He heard a slight growling sound and saw her put her hand to her stomach. Shit, he never thought to feed her; she must be starving. He grimaced at his own stupidity.

"Hungry?" he asked. "I could make you a sandwich, if you like." He stood away from the dresser and began to head toward the door.

"Please," she responded softly.

Sean was only gone about ten minutes and returned with a turkey sandwich with lettuce and mayo, just the way he remembered she liked it, and a glass of milk for her. He handed it all to her and perched against the dresser again and watched her. She ate every bite and drank the entire glass of milk. Damn, she sure was hungry, he thought. "Better?"

"Much, thank you. It smelled and tasted delicious," she told him. "I need to use the bathroom again." She got up from the bed and started to walk toward the door.

He allowed her some privacy this time without

question, and they returned to the room. He gave her space, not too much, but enough.

She sat on the side of the bed as he stood in the doorway. "Will you take that mask off for me?" she asked, raising her eyebrows at him.

"Are you sure you want me to do that?" he asked her with a nervous grit he was sure she could have noticed. He knew she must have figured it out. Bringing the picture was a good idea. "If I do that, you have to promise not to freak out."

"Please just take it off. I need to know." She twisted her hands together in her lap.

Sean took a deep breath and slowly reached up and peeled the mask off, all the while he tried to keep his eyes on her. He was ready for anything, any reaction she would throw at him. Distance was safe.

The mask came off, and he heard Jenn gasp. Hurt, pain, and anger all flashed over her face.

"Sean! Why?" She shot off the bed and rushed him. Stopping in front of him, she lean into him and started to sob. "Why, why, why…?" Her body was trembling as she slapped his chest weakly and cried.

Sean could feel prickles of tears form in his own eyes from the hurt he had caused this woman, his sweet, beautiful Jenn. He could feel each sob she produced, every tremble her body made. He reached his arms around her and took it all in. He didn't stop her from hitting him. He knew he deserved that and much, much more. He wanted to comfort her. "Shh, Jenn, I am sorry. I am so, so sorry."

Jenn slipped through his arms and dropped to the floor in front of him, sobbing and shaking.

Sean reached down, picked Jenn up, and cradled her to his chest. He carried her over to the bed and sat down, comforting her. Sure, he had regrets in his life, but this one was the biggest. How was he going to make this up to her? He sure had a lot of explaining to do, and then he had to get them both out of his father's domain. He needed to get them both to safety, and soon. "Oh, Jenn, I never meant for any of this to happen. If I could take it all back, I would." He started with his explanation while rocking her back and forth, rubbing her back, trying to calm her. "I am sorry Jake hurt you. I am sorry I hurt you those few years ago. I never meant to leave you alone. I hoped you would find someone, a friend of sorts. I loved you so much. I always did, but I didn't want you to get caught up in all this shit." Damn it was hard to get it all out, to express his feelings, to expose himself to her.

He heard her hiccup and sniffle, her sobs beginning to slow, and she shook less. He continued. At least she was listening. "My father is a very dangerous man, and he is out for revenge. You see, you are a key part in his pathetic game he considers revenge." He blew out a deep breath. The more he talked, the lighter his chest began to feel. He had been holding all his father's shit in for so long, and he was done. No more.

"Revenge," she whispered softly, looking up at him. "Revenge for what? I didn't do anything to your father."

She was biting her lip so hard he noticed that the split in it had started to bleed again. He wanted to kill his brother for hurting her. The anger he held for him was undeniable.

"The revenge is against your father, Jenn." He looked deep into her eyes, those beautiful blue eyes he would never forget. He moved one hand up her body and began to stroke her soft auburn hair. "Your father killed one of my father's men, and the way my father fixes things is with revenge. Please don't tell me you don't remember?" He raised his eyebrows in question. "I brought that photo in hopes that you would remember. Your mother, her death, do you remember?"

After a quick look of thought she responded. "My mother was murdered. I saw it happen."

"I know." He sighed. "Your father stole from mine, and the price paid was the death of your mother," he said sadly, and a tear spilled from his eye.

"Your father had my mother killed?" she shrilled. She sat up fast and moved from his lap. "All these years, I thought it was just a robbery gone wrong. You mean to say, my mother's death is my father's fault?" She was getting angry now, her voice rising

"I am sorry, Jenn, but yes. I didn't want to believe it, but my father has old crappy video footage of proof for back then and for even now. I have never seen it myself, but it has been mentioned. Your father recently murdered his right-hand man, and now my father wants revenge again." He stood from the bed, breathing deeply in frustration and started to pace the room. "He usually would want you dead, you know 'eye for an eye.' But when a file is started, sometimes he likes to play a game of sorts then the end game is left up to him. Once I learned who the mark was, and what the whole situation was, I couldn't let anything happen to you. I never wanted to hurt you, Jenn. As I said, my father is a very dangerous man. He made me take this job, but I knew I couldn't complete it like he wanted." He let out a deep breath, a relief of getting that mouthful out.

She began pacing the room. "I need to leave. Let me out of here."

"I can't just let you leave. He will hunt you down, and

that will be a worse fate than where we are now. His game is in play, and I don't know all his plans." He went to the door to prevent her from running. "And especially now that you know, you are not safe out there, not alone. If you will trust me, I will keep you safe." He stood in the doorway, bracing in the frame, hoping she didn't charge at him.

She laughed. "You will keep me safe?" Her voice started to rise. "The shit that has already happened so far. Look at me! Your own brother did this. One I had never met, I might add. Like, what the fuck, Sean. Ahhh!" she yelled.

"I can't tell you how sorry I truly am. Like I said my father is a very dangerous man, a very controlling one at that. He always told me that he held my life in his hands. He made me weak. But no more." He sighed. "If I had let either of my brothers take on this job, lord only knows what would have happened to you. I wouldn't be able to live with myself." He shoved his hands through his thick dirty-blonde hair, frustrated. "I am going to do everything in my power now to keep you from my father. You don't deserve this. It was your father's mistake, so he should pay, not you. Not my sweet little Jenn." He realized his slip of calling her sweet and little immediately. He just hope she didn't call him on it.

"How are you going to do that?" she asked him. "You just told me if I run, he'll find me."

"I will not let you run alone. With me by your side, I will do my best to protect you. Plus, I was the one watching you the past few weeks. I am pretty sure there are none of his other men staking you out. But you need to know that once we run, both of our lives are on the line." He shifted his jaw back and forth a couple times. "Can you handle that?"

"Up until you disappeared on me, Sean, you were my absolute everything. Things are different now. You are different. I don't know how much I can trust you, especially with my life."

He walked over to her, reached out, and grabbed for her hands. He was thankful she let him hold them. "Please, let me prove myself. Let me be that man again. I want to be that man again," he begged.

"Okay, I will try." She agreed with a little nod.

That made Sean breathe easier. Knowing that she was willing, made him get a move on. He had no idea what was going on in her head, but he was sure she would let him know when they had more time. He moved over to the dresser, picked up the knapsack from the floor, and began to repack Jenn's belongings. He grabbed the locket and admired it a moment before he put it in the bag. Lastly, he took the photo from the bed and packed it as well. The only thing he left out was a pair of running shoes, a pair of dark blue jeans, and shirt for her to put on. "Get dressed. We need to get out of here," he told her, zipping up the bag.

Everything was moving fast now that she had agreed to try. He was so thankful that she had a heart of gold and was able to set everything aside. She was always a smart girl, and sticking together was a smart thing right now. Getting away from his father was a good thing, but it was not going to be easy. He turned away so she could dress.

Sean hung the bag over his shoulder and headed out of the room once he noticed Jenn was ready. He went to his own room with Jenn traveling right behind. He grabbed a bag of his own and packed some clothes, a stash of cash, and his personal hygiene items. When she was not looking, he reached further in a dresser drawer and pulled out his gun and some extra ammo, and quickly shoved it in his bag. He needed something else for protection besides his fists. He grabbed his keys, cell phone, and wallet, reached for her hand, and they both jogged down the hall and out of the house.

Once in the car, buckled in, both of them breathing heavily, Jenn spoke. "Where are we going?" She looked over at him.

"As far away from here as we can. I have some cash, and I'll stop and take some money out before we leave town. I promise you, Jenn, I will do everything I can to keep you safe." He looked over at her and smiled. He put the car in gear, put his foot down hard on the pedal, and sped off.

Chapter Eight

They stopped at the nearest ATM, and they both secured as much cash as they could.

"I have cash at my house," Jenn stated. "Stop by there. The more we have, the better, right?"

Sean drove them there, and Jenn ran in. With a quick look over, she didn't notice anything out of place, but she knew that her space had been invaded, and it still hurt her. She tried to shake those feelings; she would get over it in time.

She gathered all her change off the counter and a large stash of cash she had in the back of her freezer. She left, hoping it wasn't going to be the last time she saw her humble home, and returned to the car. She buckled her seat belt back up, and they drove off.

It was eleven at night, and they had been driving for about an hour. Jenn had no idea where they were going, but it seemed like Sean had a plan. She looked over at him. He was looking pretty tired, and so was she.

"Should we stop for the night?" she asked.

"Not yet. We aren't far enough away. I don't feel comfortable enough to do it."

"But you look exhausted, Sean." She reached her hand

over and touched his shoulder.

He quickly looked over at her and smiled. Exhaustion was clearly noticeable in his eyes. "Just a little further and we will stop," he told her.

She noticed that Sean was checking the mirrors every few minutes, possibly to make sure they were not being followed. There were few other cars out at this time, but none were suspicious or followed them at any turn they made. This she knew, because she was watching her mirror, too.

They drove for another hour with no signs of being followed. Sean pulled up to the next motel, and they got a room. It was on the ground floor for easy escape if they needed one. Sean retrieved the bags from the car, and they went to the room.

The room appeared old fashioned in style and had a musty smell. It had muted brown walls that looked clean enough. The single queen-sized bed had an old faded quilt on it. The night stands on each side of the bed were dark brown with yellow lamps with tassels, and the brown shag-like carpet had small stains on it. There was a small, rickety table with a small, old television on it, and just off to the right of that was a tiny bathroom that consisted of an off-white pedestal sink, a toilet covered with filth, and a single stand-up shower. Not a place to swoon over, but would do in a pinch.

Jenn looked around the room and took it all in. "One bed for the two of us?" she murmured.

"That was all they had left for the ground floor, sorry." He tilted his head, set the bags down, and sat on the end of the bed. "Did you want to shower before you go to sleep?"

"That would be great, thanks." She took her bag and went to the small bathroom.

Jenn was pretty tired, so she didn't take her time in the shower. She washed quickly, shampooed her hair, skipping the conditioner, and got out. She towel dried and put on a pair of yellow flannel pajama pants she found in her bag and a white tank top. She repacked her bag and went back out to join Sean, after brushing her teeth and hair.

When she entered the room, Sean was sitting on the bed. He was watching country music videos on the tiny television. He was counting the money and singing along to the music with a low voice.

She set her bag down in a chair, alerting Sean she was in the room, and he stopped singing.

"Don't let me interrupt you." She giggled. "You were sounding pretty good." She was flirting, at a time like this. She supposed being around him stirred up old feelings.

"Feel better?" he looked up at her and asked.

"Very much, thank you."

"I am going to go have a quick one. Do you mind?" He got up from the bed and grabbed his bag.

"Have at it." Waving him out of the room, she smiled as she walked over to the bed and sat down. She pulled her legs up and laid down on her side and shut her eyes, allowing sleep to take her, even if it was only for a few short hours.

She was just dozing off when she felt a dip in the bed. She pretended to sleep. Her adrenaline rush was gone and fatigue was setting in. She didn't really want to talk right then. She needed to process everything. She was mad at him for the situation they were in; but in a way, she understood, too.

"Good night, my sweet Jenn," he whispered into her ear. "Nothing I do or say can ever say how sorry I am for what is happening right now, but I will make it right. I promise you that." He rolled back over.

Lying in such close proximity to Sean, Jenn's old feelings for him really began to resurface. She started to get a little tingle inside, and memories arose when she closed her eyes. She had loved this man since she was eight years old. They had been through so much together. He was her rock, her heart, her world. But now, after the years she had not seen or heard from him, here he was, the same man, but different. She tried to push the feelings aside. Now was not the time to desire or want. It didn't matter that he was spread out beside her in the same bed. She had to shake those thoughts. Trying hard, she had to fight herself from reaching out and touching him, from rolling over and kissing him on the cheek. It didn't matter that she was mad at him; she still felt what she felt and needed to rein it in. She closed her eyes tighter and thought of puppy dogs and butterflies. She really needed to get some sleep if she planned on getting through the next day.

Jenn was warm, a little too warm. She opened her eyes to a bright room; it was morning. The air she breathed was not warm, but her body was. She glanced down to see an arm wrapped around her torso. She noticed how peaceful Sean looked while asleep, curled up next to her, holding her. Jenn had always longed for this, to be held by him. Being wrapped in his arms felt amazing, but now wasn't the time. "Psst, Sean." She tried to get his attention. She used her free arm and reached over and poked his shoulder. "Sean, wake up." Still nothing, so she tried to wiggle away from him, but she didn't get far. Every time she moved, he just pulled her back in close. That made her giggle.

"It's been a long time since I have heard that." Sean

yawned, moved his arm, and stretched.

She giggled again because she couldn't help herself. "It has been a long time since I have done it." She smiled at him and sat up in the bed now that she was free of him. "You had a hold of me and would not let me go. I poked you and still you wouldn't let me go, and you just looked so damn cute when you were sleeping, I couldn't contain myself."

"I looked cute, did I?" He winked. "Since when does a grown man look cute?" He reached over for her, grabbed her by her arm, and tugged. He pulled her down and started to tickle her.

She was laughing so hard, her side hurt. He remembered every spot to touch that got to her. He used to tickle her when they were younger. She used to love that. The laughter tears had started, and her bladder was beginning to warn her. "Stop," she shouted. "I have to pee." And she tried to break free from his hold, but was having no luck. She was kicking, slapping, nothing was working. "Sean Michael Green, if you don't stop right this minute I will piss my pants, damn it." That made him stop. She got up and ran to the bathroom to relieve herself. She could hear him laughing behind her.

"Using full names is illegal, Jennifer Amelia Samos." He continued to laugh.

She yelled from the bathroom. "Well, did you want me to pee in my pants? I so would have, you know." She was laughing in the bathroom. "I do remember the time you made me do it once. You were a big jerk that day."

"Holy shit, you remember that." He stopped laughing.

"How can I forget the day I pissed my pants in front of a boy? I was horrified. But you made it seem like nothing. Like it was okay. You were always there for me then." She spoke as she walked from the bathroom. "I remember everything about us. You were my world, Sean. I was so mad when you left me."

"I'm sorry, Jenn. I thought it was for the best. Can you ever forgive me?"

She stopped at the end of the bed and looked at him. "You have a few years to make up for, but I think with time, I might be able to forgive you. That is, if we survive your father."

***

Sean was thankful that Jenn didn't hate him for everything that was happening. He just hoped he could do as he promised. He would do everything he could to keep her safe, even if his own life was lost in the process, but he wouldn't tell her that.

Sean knew they couldn't stay at the motel. They had to get farther away from Santa Monica, farther away from his father. If they had any chance of surviving, their key goal was distance.

He walked over to her and pulled her into a tight hug. He wrapped his arms around her, and he didn't want to let go. "We need to get ready to hit the road." He stepped back but didn't release her. He kept his hands on her shoulders and looked down at her and grinned.

"I understand." She looked up at him with a small smile.

They both packed up their bags and loaded them into the car. After one quick stop at a gas station, the gas tank full and a few snacks and drinks bought, they hit the freeway to their next destination.

They had been driving for an hour. Sean noticed Jenn was quiet. She wasn't paying much attention to where they were heading. But when he drove past a familiar place, the

Shark Reef Aquarium, she spoke up.

"Vegas?" she turned toward him and asked. "You think your father won't find us here?"

He glanced at her. "Dad's associates don't reach this far. So, I don't think we will be recognized. But we will still change up our looks. Plus, we need a big city to blend in with." He grinned playfully at her. "And while we are here, maybe we can have a little fun." He faced back toward the road and continued to drive. They drove until they reached the Fremont. Sean pulled into an underground parking garage across from the hotel.

"Seriously?" She looked at him wide-eyed. She shook her head, unbuckled, and descended from the car.

Sean chuckled. "Relax, I know you think I am crazy, but this is a great place." He walked around the car, grabbed the bags from the popped trunk, and led Jenn out of the garage. Sean nudged her and gave her a grin. He wanted to get her smiling again. He knew bringing her to Vegas would bring back childhood memories, and even though they were supposed to be in hiding, and they would sort of be disguised, what would be the harm in making new memories.

Even though they were pretty booked solid, the hotel still had one room left, the honeymoon suite. He hoped she wouldn't freak out about the bed situation again. Especially when they had the opportunity of using all the luxuries at a very cheap price.

Once checked in and situated in the room, Sean told Jenn he was going out. That he was going to the store to grab some supplies for changing their looks.

He wasn't gone long. Returning with a few bags containing hair dye, temporary colored contacts, and sunglasses. Setting everything on the bed, he called Jenn over. Looking at her, he spoke. "So I tried to think of things that would change us the most. I got hair dye, brown and black. Choose which you would like. And I got us green and brown contacts." He looked up at her with a grimace.

Biting her lip and browsing through all the products, Jenn looked to him and responded. "I think I will take the black dye and the green contacts."

Sean nodded and handed her the chosen products. Jenn took the dye and contacts and headed to the bathroom, with Sean following suit once she was done.

An hour later, both of them were sporting new hair and eye colors. Neither could believe how different they looked.

Sean thought that it was about time they went and got something to eat. He needed to keep his strength up, just in case. But, with traveling the distance they did and making it out of his father's region alive, he had his fingers crossed that they could try and relax a little.

"Hey, Jenn, do you feel comfortable enough to leave the hotel to get something to eat?"

"I don't think that's a great idea." She bit her lip with a look of indecision. "Are you sure it's safe?"

"Yes. My father's dealings don't reach this far. I am one hundred percent sure he has no associates here. We should be good to at least get some dinner," he answered as he headed toward the door with the key card. "So, you ready to eat?"

Jenn chewed on her lip for a minute, then she nodded. "Okay, sure. Let's do this. I am starved." They left the room and hit the elevator.

Chapter Nine

Connor Green knew he couldn't trust his son. He wished he could, but when it came to that little woman, he knew his boy would be weak. Sean and Jenn were on the move. The tracking system on his computer was showing a little red blip on the screen; they had just left the house. He had hoped his son would not be stupid. He had explained what would happen if he disobeyed him. He supposed the hunt would be on for not just one head but two. He loved his son, but he just never learned. Convincing that young lad, Joey, two years ago to seduce little Jenn and gift her with a locket that contained a tracking device was one of the smartest things he had done. Now he could find them wherever they decided to run. The thought made him smile widely.

Connor had given them a few days of respite. He thought it was time to check if they had settled anywhere. He booted up his computer, opened the application that was connected to the tracker in the locket, and waited for their location to be found. Las Vegas. "Fucking figures," he mumbled. If his dimwit son thought that was far enough away, he was wrong. Time to send some reinforcements. He wondered if Jake would suffice. He knew what the girl looked like, and he had a take-no-prisoners' attitude. He picked up his phone. "Jake, they are in Vegas. Get on it." He listened for a moment to see if his son would disagree, which he did not, and hung up. Sean had fucked up, so now the body count would increase.

***

Jake arrived in Vegas on his father's orders, but he was not alone. He brought along Simon. Simon was one of his father's more fierce and unknown lackeys. He knew that his brother fucked up. Jake didn't want to be the one to deal with him, but he had no problem dealing with the girl.

His father told him the last location the tracker placed Sean and Jenn was somewhere just off the strip, so they drove around for a bit until they decided to just hit up each hotel in the surrounding area until they found them.

It took longer than he expected. Jake was thankful that his stupid brother didn't even seem to try to hide; he used his real name. The damn Fremont for God's sake. At least he would blend in with the crowd.

Now that he knew where they were, he needed to make a plan to eliminate the targets. He and Simon didn't want Sean knowing they were found, so they left to bunk in an even cheaper hotel down the way.

***

It had been two days since they hit Vegas and there hadn't been a single sign that Sean's father's men followed them. He knew they couldn't stay in Vegas for too long. His father would send someone after them at some point. There was no doubt about that. For now he needed to open up to Jenn and give her a few days to grasp the reality of everything, then he would make plans to move on. Finding a way to get new identities was on his to-do list, but it would wait for now.

By being able to breathe a bit better and somewhat relax, Sean thought Jenn would able to try and piece together the puzzle of the past and understand why her father would betray his family.

That morning they were sitting by the open window having coffee, taking in the sites of tourists milling around the area. Sean knew by the look on her face that Jenn had something to say, so he sat patiently and waited for her to open up.

She set her mug down and looked over at him and smiled. "So, Sean, you say my mother was murdered by your father?" she questioned, a casual tone to her voice.

Sean set his cup down, turned his body in his chair toward her, and grinned. He wanted to be honest with her. He wanted to tell her all that he knew of the situation. Taking a deep breath and blowing it out, he started. "Yes, Jenn, my father killed your mother. Well, truth be told, he had her killed." Sean tipped his head down, feeling defeated. He knew she needed some closure, or at least answers, to come to terms with this. He hated knowing what the answers would mean for her. "Apparently your father got a little close"—he looked up into her eyes—"too close to the drugs my father was selling. And my father didn't like that." Sean leaned into the table. "Dad gave him several attempts to come clean about it, but when your dad began to use the drugs, stealing them and lie about it, I guess Dad wouldn't tolerate it anymore. Your father was warned but didn't heed that warning." Sean put his head in his hands and sighed.

Jenn listened, but she seemed to not believe what she had heard. "He ignored a warning? A warning that could have saved my mother?" she whispered.

Sean could only nod in response. He knew she was

going to break soon. If she was anything like she was when they were kids, she would snap anytime. Her heart was big and soft, and he knew it.

She suddenly stood up from her chair, grabbed her mug, and threw it against the wall by the patio door. It smashed and crumbled to the ground. "Why?" she screamed. "Why the fuck did he ignore such a thing?" She began to pace. "I fucking hate him!" she gritted out. Falling to her knees, she began to sob. Her hands in her hair, she pulled. She was trembling, her emotions fully overwhelming her.

Sean wasn't sure if she would accept his touch, his comfort, but he went to her anyway. He knelt down and wrapped his arms around her. Well, at least he tried. She pushed him off and sprang up.

"And you..." she cried. "Why are you doing all this?" Pacing once again. "Why did you kidnap me? Why now?" She began to cry as she paced.

Sean leaned against the wall with his arms crossed. He felt helpless in consoling her, so he guessed answering her questions would have to do.

"Can you please try to calm down, Jenn?" He wanted her to relax, needed her to see reason.

"Fuck you, Sean!" She stopped and spat at him. "Tell me what the hell is going on."

Sean wiped the spit off. "Jenn, please," he begged.

"Please what, Sean?" She growled. "You fucking break into my home, drug me, kidnap me, and lock me up." She walked by the table with a vase of flowers on it, grabbed it and whipped it him.

He barely managed to duck from the flying vase; it just missed his head. She still had good aim, he thought. He had taught her well. "You don't understand. I had to take this job." He slowly followed her around the room, attempting to reason with her, wanting her to understand.

She stopped and stared at him. She was breathing heavy. "You had to take the job?" she gritted out. "Please explain why you had to take this job. Enlighten me, Sean!"

He almost bumped into her when she stopped, so Sean backed up a bit to give her space. He sighed. "Yes, I had to, Jenn. I already told you." He slumped his shoulders in defeat. "If I didn't, my father would have sent one of my brothers or one of the other men, and lord only knows how things would have turned out," he explained. "I took the job to protect you. My father may have killed you."

She laughed. A full-out laugh. "To protect me? How is kidnapping me protecting me?" She turned and went to the bathroom.

Sean began to follow, and Jenn realized this. She turned and spoke. "I need a fucking moment." She turned back, went in the bathroom, slammed the door, and locked it.

Chapter Ten

Sean was sitting on the bed when Jenn came out of the bathroom, her eyes puffy and red. Her skin was pale white and she looked tired. Her short jean shorts were rumpled and her blue tank top was damp, probably from the tears she shed. She walked over and sat beside Sean on the bed and leaned against him. Resting her head on his shoulder, she sighed in defeat.

"I'm sorry, Sean," she whispered.

Sean tipped his head down to her, reached up with a hand, and raised her head up by the chin with his index finger to meet eye to eye. "What do you have to be sorry for, babe?"

Jenn blinked several times to hold the tears back and bit her lip. With all the emotions swimming deep inside of her of the past events they shared and the present situation, she wasn't sure how to handle everything. She wanted to be strong. But she also wanted to trust and depend on this man, her first love. When she heard 'babe' her heart melted just a little. That piece of endearment helped her see the man in front of her. Her friend. She relished in that feeling.

"This is just so much to take in." Jenn sat up, but sustained to keep eye contact with him. Taking a deep breath, she continued. "I never thought my father could be the man that you are saying. Being the cause of such damage and hurt in my life." She crossed her arms across her chest and squeezed as if trying to hold herself together. "Why would he do this? I just don't understand."

Jenn looked at him with an expression of pain. She laid her feelings out there, freely for him to see, hoping he understood. She hadn't felt so lost since her mother died.

Placing his hands in his lap, he let out a slow breath. "I wish I could answer every single question you have, babe, but I only know what I know." Sean licked his lips and continued. "Once your father got into the drugs, he just seemed to, you know, change."

Jenn suddenly scrunched her eyebrows together in a quick rush of rage. "I fucking know he changed, Sean! I just didn't think it was because of drugs. I thought it was gambling or something easier to deal with," she yelled. She moved herself back from him and put her hands on her thighs. "I just want to fucking know how he could do this to his fucking wife, to me!"

Sean reached out and took her hands in his. "Shh, baby, try and calm down." He moved closer to her on the bed and put one arm around her shoulder and pulled her closer to him. "I can't answer for him. I wish I could. All I can do now is try and help you through it all." He tucked her head down to his chest and kissed the top of her head. He began to rock them slightly back and forth on the bed.

The soothing action was something she used to like when she was younger, and she could feel the tension leave her body. She was glad Sean remembered the little tidbit about her.

"Babe?"

"Yes?"

"You hungry?"

"Little bit, yeah."

Sean chuckled and ease Jenn from his grip. She was sitting up and facing him. He leaned in and kissed her forehead.

"Let's get some grub then, yeah?" Sean smiled.

"Sounds good. Can I just freshen up first?"

"You look great, babe."

Jenn scowled at that. She knew she did not look anywhere near good, not nice, not even close to looking alive. She knew her clothes were a mess, and her face—well she could only imagine.

"Don't start fucking lying to me. I know I look like shit," she snarled and waltzed to the bathroom to get ready.

When Jenn came from the bathroom, she wore a purple, low-cut three-quarter sleeved shirt that was formed to her body and blue jean capris. She was refreshed and ready to eat. She looked up at the sound of Sean clearing his throat and smiled while moving toward him.

"You ready?" he asked.

"I am." She stopped right in front of him and looked into his eyes. She noted the glimmer of desire there and bit her lip. She began to feel a slight tingle in her groin, something she hadn't felt in a long time.

Sean reached up and released her lip from her teeth, gently caressing her bottom lip with his index finger. He reached around her torso with his other hand and pulled her closer to him, his eyes never leaving hers. "Jenn..."

Jenn put her hands on his chest, her breathing and heart rate increasing as lust surged through her body. "Yes?" she breathed out.

He leaned in and crushed his lips with hers and dug

his hand into her hair.

Jenn felt his tongue teasing her lips, seeking an opening, so she gave it to him and gave her all in return. When his tongue met hers, she moaned and the kiss went deeper. She felt Sean pull her tighter to him, and it was as if every cell in her body came to life. A fire was ignited within, a heat she never felt before. Every wisp of the tongue, every nip of the lip, every moan, every groan, she returned with ignited fire. She couldn't get enough of him. She had wanted this kiss since she was a teenager.

He slid his lips to the corner of her mouth, then her chin, and proceeded with open-mouthed kisses down her neck.

Jenn tipped her head freely to give access and went limp in his arms momentarily, enjoying every second of it.

Sean's hand moved from her back down to her ass and squeezed. His kisses moved along her collarbone.

Feeling the ass grab, reality sank in, and the lusty fog lifted. She gave him a nudge back mid moan. "Sean." She exhaled and rested her arms on his chest.

Sean stepped back a little. He moved his hands to her shoulders and took a few slow deep breathes. "Wow, sorry." He shook his head. "I just couldn't help myself there, Jenn. You look amazing, and…" He shut his eyes tight and then opened them, blowing out a puff of air. "Fuck, I have wanted to do that for years, and I just couldn't let the moment pass." He gave her a pathetic excuse of a puppy-dog-eyed look.

Jenn just chuckled, gave him a light thump in the chest, and turned. "Let's just go eat."

Sean grabbed her wrist mid turn. "Seriously, Jenn, I am sorry."

"It's okay, Sean." She bit her lip, looked away shyly,

and muttered, "I wanted it, too." She walked over to the table by the door, grabbed her purse and the key card. "Coming?"

"Yeah."

She opened the door and walked out.

Chapter Eleven

They ended up staying in the hotel to eat. The bar just off the casino had just what they both were craving, wings. Hot, mild, buffalo-style, you name it, they had it, and Jenn was going to make sure to have her fill.

They sat in a booth overlooking the casino. The lights and sounds were very intriguing to Jenn. She never had been overly adventurous in her adult life. Jenn was eager to try something new. "After we eat can we go test our luck?" She raised her eyebrows and bit her lip, hoping Sean would agree. They may be on the run and in hiding, but a little fun wouldn't hurt, at least she hoped. They did look different now with the new hair and eye color, not so easily recognizable, so she had her fingers crossed.

Sean looked over his shoulder, then back at her. He scratched his chin, then smirked. "Sure we can, babe."

Jenn squealed in delight. She had never been to a casino before, and if she could escape the shitstorm they were in for just a moment, then she would.

After a dozen hot wings and the large order of garlic bread between them was gone, they used the facilities and entered the casino for their so-called fun times.

A few drinks in, Jenn was having a blast on the slots.

She had spent only about twenty dollars and was up ten. She had never felt such a thrill in her dull life. Taking another sip of her Black Cherry Vanilla Coke, infused with sweet vanilla-flavored vodka, she slotted a few more coins and pulled the lever.

Ding, ding went the bells, winning the small jackpot again. Sean turned from his machine and laughed. "I sure wish I had your luck, babe. I haven't won a damn thing." He leaned into her and kissed her on the cheek. Jenn blushed bashfully, or maybe it was just the alcohol, she wasn't sure.

"You just need to try a different machine." She giggled. Now that was definitely the alcohol. Jenn didn't have much to giggle about lately, but with the alcohol running through her system, she felt like the stress of the situation was lifted from her shoulders. She felt safe and free at the moment and was enjoying it.

"You okay for a few minutes, babe? I need to take a leak." He set his bucket of coins on her side table.

"Yes, sir." She looked up at him and gave him a serious look. "Remember, if you shake it more than twice, you are playing with it." She couldn't hold the serious look for long, a giggle burst out.

Sean smirked and let out a small laugh, then looked at Jenn pointedly. "The only playing…" He narrowed his eyes at her and a sexy smirk arose on his mouth. "The only playing will be with you, in our room, babe, not in the bathroom." He turned and left her to her slots.

Jenn was shocked at how blunt he was about the sexual innuendo, but it didn't really bother her. She wanted that more than anything. All the old feelings stirred deep inside of her with the alcohol flowing, making her inhibitions weak and her desire for him stronger. She turned back to her machine and slotted more coins.

She had just pulled the lever on the machine when a chill went up her spine. A strange feeling like she was being watched. Slowly, she looked around, but didn't see anyone looking in her direction. Not that it was easy to tell, with the casino being as busy as it was at the time.

She tried to shake off the sensation and resumed her game, but the feeling got more intense. Goose bumps rose on her neck and arms. She looked up and around the room again a little slower. This time she did notice someone looking at her, and she gasped. She didn't know the man, but there was just something about him that was semi-familiar. The man had an evil glare on his face, his eyes were dark, and he snarled. He was a few machines away, sitting at a table. He didn't move; he just stared at her.

Jenn quickly looked around for Sean. He was nowhere to be seen. Fear crept through her. She wasn't sure why the man was staring at her, and she didn't want to wait around to find out.

She grabbed both buckets of coins and her purse and headed in the direction of the restrooms. She hoped she would run into him along the way. The feeling of the creepy eyes watching her remained while she tried to walk calmly. She wasn't going to get rid of that feeling until she was locked in the room with Sean.

Jenn was scared, and with the alcohol in her system, her limbs trembled while she walked. She bumped into people as she went and when a pair of strong arms grabbed her she just about freaked out.

"Jenn, whoa, where you are going, babe?" Sean looked around and back to her. "Babe, you are safe. What happened?" He pulled her into a hug and kissed the top of her head.

"A m-man," she stuttered.

"What man?"

Jenn pointed back to where they were playing slots with her free hand, her other hand and arm holding the buckets of change. "Back there. He was staring at me."

"Babe, he was probably looking at something else."

Jenn looked up at Sean, tears brimming her eyes. "No, Sean, he was looking at me. He looked somewhat familiar too. I don't know from where, but he was creepy. He just stared." A chill ran through her body. "It freaked me out, okay? Can we just go back to the room, please?" she pleaded.

Sean curled her into his body, walked with her over to cash in their coins, and they went to their room.

Once in their room, Jenn was a little calmer. Sean released his hold on her and looked down at her with a concerned expression. "Are you okay now?"

Jenn took a deep, calming breath, licked her lips and nodded at him. "It's just with everything going on..." She stepped back from him. "My emotions are so jumbled about the situation, and about you." She turned and walked toward the bed. She sat on the edge and removed her shoes while still trying to get her thoughts out. "I just don't know what to do, or what to say, or even how to react. Everything is just… I don't know what or who to trust." She bit her lip and looked up at him through her long lashes.

He walked to her and knelt in front of her, taking her hands in his. He looked up at her. "Please, I beg you, Jenn." He pulled her hands up to his mouth and kissed them. "I beg for your forgiveness. I went about this all the wrong way. I have been locked in my father's grasp for years, and when you, or rather your file, was presented to me, I faltered. I didn't know what to do, how to fix it." He bowed his head in her lap and took a few deep breathes.

Jenn was confused, but her feelings for this broken man were busting to get out. Pushing her fear aside, letting the whole scary scenario that muddled her mind of truths and lies go for just a little while, she listened to him plead for forgiveness for his wrong doings. She pulled a hand from his grasp and put it on his head. Running her fingers through his unruly hair, she could feel his hot breath on her jean-clad legs, the warmth soaking right into her. Her skin began to tingle, her nerve endings coming alive. "Sean," she whispered and tugged on his hair lightly, allowing lust to overpower her fear.

He took a few more deep breaths and looked up at her. Sean moved his hands up her thighs to her hips and pulled her closer to the edge of the bed; she gasped. He shifted her legs apart and shuffled closer to her without losing eye contact. "Jennifer, I will never be able to make up for what I have done, for my past, or for leaving you behind."

She interrupted him by raising a hand and shushing him with a finger, placing it in front of his supple lips. "Shh…" She let the words hang. With fire burning through her veins, heat surging around her body from his simple touch, she was in no state of mind for explanations. Her fear buried itself and allowed her to feel the lust that she had been denied for years. She didn't want to be afraid now, she only wanted one thing, him. The feel of his lips, his hands, and his muscular body. She wanted him to do everything she had ever dreamed of since she first learned about sex and the extent of its pleasure.

She moved both hands to his face and cupped his jaw, licking her lips. She began to tremble. She was never the one to initiate a kiss of this magnitude. She leaned down as she pulled him toward her.

He crushed his lips to hers. Lips moving sensually, with passion, lust. He licked her bottom lip and then nibbled. In one swift motion, he moved to gently lay Jenn back on the bed while ravishing her mouth.

She opened for him, and he swooped his tongue. The kiss went deeper. Jenn groaned in pleasure. The man could kiss, that was for sure. A thrill ignited within her. She felt alive, sexy, and she wanted this. She wanted him. She moved her hands through his hair, messing it more and then down his neck and tried to pull him closer. She heard him moan. Tipping her head back, she needed to catch her breath. "Oh God."

He caressed her torso, one hand pulling on the sleeve of her shirt and the other cupped her breast. He moved his mouth down her chin, rapidly breathing along the way, suckling and nipping down her throat. "Fuck, Jenn." He growled. "You taste amazing." He continued down to her collarbone.

He moved his one hand to her half-bared breast and kneaded it. His other hand moved over and pulled the sleeve down as he licked and teased every part of her naked flesh as he went.

It had never felt like this with her last boyfriend. She couldn't even remember his name at the moment. She couldn't remember much of anything. All she could do was feel. Her skin felt alive and every touch of his wet tongue was making her nerves dance with pleasure. She never wanted it to stop. She arched her back up into him, offering herself to his wanting mouth, expressing her need while she breathed heavily and moaned deeply. "More!"

He growled. "Fuck, babe, I will give you everything you need. I will make you scream, like you have never screamed before." He immediately sat up, puffing out lusty breaths, grasped the shirt between her breasts, and ripped. He tore the shirt away and dove right back in. He palmed both breasts, and took one nipple into his mouth and sucked. He sucked until it peaked, then licked around it before moving to the other and lavishing it with equal measure. "A-fuckin-mazing," he mumbled while teasing the now taut pink flesh.

Jenn felt like she was in heaven. All this pleasure surging through her. She brought her hands up to his head, gripped his hair, and rubbed it around. She wasn't sure what to do, but just went with what felt right. It was as if her hands had a mind of their own. She wasn't sure what to expect from him, but she definitely wanted it all.

He continued lavishing her with wet kisses down her stomach, caressing her along the way. He reached her navel, licked around it and then dipped his tongue inside and groaned. He brought his hands to the waist of her capris and then peeked to look up at her.

After her body involuntarily bucked again from his pleasing contact, she realized he had stopped at her pants. She quickly looked down at him and saw the look in his eyes. The lust, the desire, and the question. He was asking for permission. She immediately nodded. "Yes," she almost yelled. She pushed herself up to a sitting position and attempted to help him, but he stopped her.

"I got this." He winked at her and proceeded to unbutton her capris, slowly pulling the zipper down. He pulled the portion of the pants apart and groaned. "Fuck, those are hot."

She was wearing a pair of black lace panties. They were bikini cut and barely covered anything. She didn't wear them for anyone in particular, they were just comfortable. But hearing him groan like that, and knowing it was for her, she felt herself get a little damper. She had never felt this desired for before. It was doing amazing things to her and her mind. She usually was somewhat timid, but with Sean, she felt like a different person when it came to sex.

"You like those, huh?" She grinned at him and wiggled her hips to tease him. She noticed him fighting for control. His breath was deep, and he just stared, and didn't touch. She knew he would break soon. She needed him to touch her.

"Take them off," she whispered, just loud enough for him to hear.

"Fucking hell, yes," he growled. He gripped her hips, lifted a little, pulled on the capris and yanked them down and off. He wasn't wasting time now. He reached for her panties, and in quick movements, her panties were shredded. He jumped off the bed. "Move up on the bed." His eyes roved over her naked flesh as he removed his own clothing is a flash. He returned to the bed and crawled up to her, spread her legs, and knelt between them.

"You are fucking gorgeous. I can't believe I let you go."

Jenn could see the honesty in his eyes. She knew it to be true. She wanted this, him, and she wanted him now. She would have to deal with their mess later. There was too much to think about, to talk about, and she was in no state of mind for that. Desire was fueling her, and sex was what she wanted. "I am here now. Whatever happened, happened. Now if you don't get the fuck on with it, I think I'll have to do it myself," she egged him on. He looked glorious in his naked state. Erect and beautiful. She had never thought a penis was attractive, never in pictures or even her ex's, but Sean's was spectacular. She tried to lean up to get closer, but he stopped her.

"No, I fucking got this, babe. My pleasure is your pleasure. I want you to feel everything I feel." He laid his hands on each of her lower legs and began to move them slowly upward. Caressing her skin, her inner and outer shin, knee, and then thigh. He moved his hands inward, one lightly stroked her groin area while the other teased her little tufts of hair. He dipped a finger into the crease of her folds; she was plenty wet. He moved his finger up and down her slit, finding her swollen clit and circling it.

Jenn's body tensed. "Oh my God, Sean, don't stop. That feels amazing." It felt like her body was doing everything on its own. It went on a joyride, and she was just hanging on. Her hips jutted up to his hand, and she moaned to his touch. She felt his finger delve into her and nerve endings that have never been touched, sprang to life. She gasped and squeezed her eyes closed. She could feel it all; it was as if he were everywhere. Suddenly, she felt hot breath between her legs and her eyes opened wide. No one had ever been down there. Her ex had been against it. His breath was hot and teasing, but he wasn't moving any closer. It was as if he were asking permission again. So she questioned him. "Sean?" She looked down at him with narrowed, lust-filled eyes.

"Your smell is driving me crazy, Jenn. I would give my last breath for just a taste. I just…" Sean breathed deeply. "I just need to know that you want this. Are you sure it is me you want?" He stared into her eyes.

Leaning up on her elbows, her eyes glistened with tears. The tears of the unknown and also of happiness of finally getting a piece of the man she had always wanted. Even if it were for one night, she would have to live with that. "More than anything."

That was all he seemed to need to hear because he had dipped his head down and lazily licked her slit from bottom to top and sucked on her clit.

"Oh fuck!" Jenn fell back on the bed. She never knew what to expect when she agreed to it, but it sure was not this. She felt like she had fallen from heaven and her wings had been clipped. She hoped Sean was there to catch her.

He lifted each leg and set it over his shoulders, then tucked his hands under her ass and lifted her up. He licked and sucked her clit. Then he pulled a hand from her ass and began to caress her slit with his fingers. Up and down, and then he dipped one finger, then two. He licked around and up and down. He slowly pumped his fingers in and out of her, and he lapped up all the juices that flowed out.

She shuddered, gripping the sheets. She bucked her hips up to his mouth. The feeling was amazing, and she never wanted it to stop. "Yes, oh yes, don't stop. Fuck, Sean." She wriggled and moaned until she felt an odd sensation build up inside, something she never felt before. She felt like she was going to burst at the seams. Her toes felt like they were curling. She gripped the sheets tighter. She bit her lip hard, squeezed her eyes closed, arched her back as much as she could with Sean holding her with his mouth, and then it was like an explosion. Bright stars shone behind her eyes, every tense muscle spontaneously relaxing like an elastic band being flung across a room. Then she screamed. She tried not to, but she just couldn't help herself. "Oh ahh, ahh, Sean!"

Sean growled and lapped up her come as she released and went limp on the bed. He kissed wet kisses up from her pussy, to her stomach, to her breasts; where he sucked each nipple in and teased them to a pleasing peak once again and continued kissing his way up to her mouth. He moved his body to lay over her's, his erection at her opening. He kissed her deeply and passionately. He nipped his way down to a sensitive spot behind her ear, and he sucked there.

Breathing a bit better and feeling extremely relaxed, she opened her eyes to look at him. By the twinkle in his eye, she knew they were far from done. She smiled at him.

"You okay?" He smirked.

"Never better." She felt a bit shy at the moment, but she pushed that aside and reached with one hand for his erection without losing eye contact. As soon as she touched his hard length, she heard him hiss. She licked her lips and looked down. She hadn't taken the time to actually take in the size of him when she'd had the chance, and she was impressed. Not that she had much to compare him to, but she had seen pictures, and he was gorgeous. She wrapped her dainty hand around his massive erection and gave a gentle squeeze. Sean hissed again and she smiled. She made him feel like that, and that made her feel powerful.

Her hands were on him, and she could tell he was struggling with his control. She stroked him once. Twice.

He took a deep breath. He reached up and moved some of the hair stuck to her forehead and tucked it behind her ear. "I wouldn't play too much, beautiful, or there won't be much action for a while. My control is weak when it comes to you." He leaned down and kissed her lips. His hand moved slowly down, caressing every inch of flesh, down until he reached her hip. He got up in a kneeling position between her legs again. Took her hand from his erection, brought it to his mouth and kissed her palm. He released her hand once he set it on the bed. He then grabbed his hard length and rubbed in her juices of her slit and groaned. "So fucking wet still."

Jenn wasn't in control, he was, and she was okay with that. All the kind words, nicknames, they made her melt even more into him. When he rubbed his erection against her, she jumped. Oh my God, it was happening. All other thoughts of life, past, present and or future went out the window. The only thing that mattered right now, was him and what he was doing to her.

"I'm clean, babe. Never gone bareback before," Sean whispered as he pulled her closer.

She didn't understand what he was talking about, why he was mentioning this. "That's good. Me too," she said, then shook her head. "I mean, I always made sure my ex wore a condom, and I'm clean too."

Sean blew out a breath. "That's good. I am saying this because we have no condoms, and I need inside you. I need to feel you, babe." He continued to tease her with his penis, rubbing up and down.

Every time he hit her clit, her body would do a little pleasing jump. "I need you, too, Sean." She moaned. He had just hit her clit and couldn't take it anymore. "I need you, now." And she reached around his hip and grabbed his ass, urging him forward.

He slid his penis up her slit, took hold of her hip, and thrust inside of her. "Fuck." He grunted pulling back slightly and thrust again. He gripped her hips with both hands and began pumping in and out. He moved his hands up her body, caressed her breasts, pinched her taut nipples, and growled his pleasure. He reached under her back and pulled her up to him. He wrapped his arms around her and continued to thrust, deep and hard.

She was loving every minute of it.

He licked his lips and pulled her head to his and crushed his mouth to hers. Forcing her mouth open with his tongue, thrusting it inside.

"Oh. My. God," Jenn panted out between thrusts. Pleasure swarmed her entire body. It had never felt like this before. What her ex did to her was fucking beans compared to this. He was no lover in comparison. Sean knew what he was doing, and he was doing it amazingly. She wrapped her arms around his neck and tipped her head back, panting. Her body bouncing with his thrusts, her breasts crushed against him, she took everything he gave. She felt her pussy clenching around him, he was hitting just the right spot.

He thrust deep and hard, groaning in her ear. "God, this feels like home."

Her body spasmed one final time, and Jenn screamed through her orgasm. She raked her nails down his back. And with one final thrust, he released his seed inside of her.

He grabbed her hair and pulled her in for a passionate kiss, deep with tongue. When they were both limp from their release, Sean pulled back. He touched her cheek softly with his fingers. "Love," was all he spoke before pulling out and laying them down. He laid her on her side and spooned her from the back. He pulled a blanket up and covered them. He wrapped his arms around her middle, and they both relaxed in the moment.

Chapter Twelve

Jenn woke to something hard poking her in the ass, and heat crept over her skin. She knew men could get hard-ons in the morning, but she didn't want to make assumptions. She wiggled her bottom a little to test the theory. She had never slept with, and then woke up next, to a man, and naked to boot. So with a little wiggle, the theory tested, and she grinned at the results.

He moaned and wrapped his arms tighter around her midriff, giving her a little squeeze. "Babe, if you keep doing that, we won't be getting out of this bed anytime soon," he whispered huskily.

Jenn settled her hands on his and turned her head a bit. "Maybe that's the idea." She bit her lip and smiled. While in his arms, she felt braver than she ever had. The longer she was with him, the faster the shy girl he once knew faded. The past years they had been apart didn't seem to matter anymore. She had always wanted him. Now she had him. And as long as Sean truly wanted her, she was going to be the woman he deserved.

She gazed into his gorgeous dark eyes. She never thought she would ever get here. She didn't want to waste any time with him, past or no past. She wanted to make up for what she had missed. She pushed her ass into him again and wiggled.

"Fuck," he growled. He pushed himself up on one arm and leaned over her. He took her mouth by surprise and he took it fast and hard. He shifted one hand down to her hip and slowly caressed her thigh.

She moaned at his touch. With thoughts of the night prior, lust swept through her. She waited patiently for what was to come next.

He lifted her naked thigh, shifted forward, and slid his erection into her. "God, Jenn, you feel so good." He thrust slowly into her. He kissed her neck and nibbled her ear. He cupped a breast in his hand and pinched the nipple, making it peak.

She felt her body clench around him, his hands on her breast giving her sensations she had only read about. She leaned her head into the pillow to give him better access to her neck. She was aware of every part of her body and mind. She felt alive. She moaned with each of his thrusts. Each one felt better than the last. She never wanted it to end. She grabbed his ass with one hand, a hint to give her more, and gripped the sheets beside her with the other. She was in sleepy pleasure overload, and she loved it.

"More," she moaned breathlessly. She heard him growl and instantly the thrusts became harder and felt deeper. She felt like she was being touched in places of the unknown. The tingly feeling in her stomach started, she felt her toes start to curl, her breathing became erratic, and she knew she was going to blow anytime.

He growled a husky sound and pumped into her with need.

Jenn gripped his ass tighter and began to pant as her orgasm built. Her body trembled with each thrust he gave.

He was hitting her G-spot, and it was driving her mad.

"Oh, fuck, Jenn, I hope you are ready because, ah, ah…" He grunted.

He pumped once, twice, and on the third he stayed embedded in her and held her tight as he growled his release.

She wasn't sure what he had done, but on that final thrust, she burst. She let go and blissfully groaned out her release just as he began his. She squeezed her eyes tight. The orgasm was even stronger than the one from the night before. She couldn't believe such a feeling existed.

She felt him lighten his hold on her as they both came down from their high. Her body was so relaxed, she didn't think she would be able to move for a while. She felt she had to say something after that, but her mind felt like mush. "Wow" was what came out, and she felt stupid, but when she felt his body shake against hers, she knew it was okay.

Sean chuckled. "Did you seriously just say 'wow'?" He slowly eased himself out of her warmth and lay on his back and chuckled again.

Jenn felt slightly embarrassed. She didn't think it was a bad word to use, but then again, she could barely think at the time she had said it. She flipped herself over onto her other side, pulled the sheet with her trying to be modest, and perched herself up on her elbow.

Unsure of herself, she whispered, "Was that not a good enough word to use? I mean, I can't think straight I'm so relaxed, but was it not the right word, or was it the sex that was not good?" She bit her lip and looked down to the bed. What if the sex wasn't good? She knew she enjoyed it, but did he?

He tipped her head up with his fingers. Looking into

her eyes, he spoke softly. "The sex was more than good, Jenn. It was fucking amazing." He ran his thumb across her pouting bottom lip. He turned onto his side and cuddled up to her.

"But you laughed, Sean. It felt like I did something wrong."

He leaned over to kiss her gently on the lips. "You did nothing wrong, said nothing wrong. It was me. I was stupid. An idiot as usual. I've just never had that kind of reaction from sex before. It threw me off my game."

"Oh."

He reached over, wrapped his arm around her shoulders, and pulled her to him. He turned to lay on his back and curled her into him so they were snuggled together. "You can never do or say anything wrong to me, Jenn. Never underestimate yourself. I'm a man, and we are dumb sometimes." He kissed the top of her head and rubbed her back in comfort.

Jenn wrapped her arm over his chiseled torso and absorbed the comfort he gave. She felt better knowing that she had done nothing wrong, and he had enjoyed the sex as much as her. Expressing feelings was new to her, and not easy.

After fifteen minutes of laying in bed, Jenn's stomach grumbled. She was embarrassed about how loud it was; she was sure Sean heard it. And she was right. She felt his body shake a little.

Sean chuckled. He ran his hand through her hair and cleared his throat. "Hungry, babe?"

Jenn pushed herself up onto her elbow, and feeling slightly embarrassed, she answered him. "Um, yeah."

"All right then, let's get cleaned up and get some grub."

Chapter Thirteen

After two days of no other incidents, Sean figured it was safe to assume Jenn's feeling of someone was watching her, was just a misunderstanding. The note he found on the floor by the door yesterday was odd. It said *'I can see you'*. It was random and could have been from anyone, to anyone. Not wanting to upset Jenn further, he didn't tell her about it. He put the note in his bag and didn't think of it again.

Feeling a little more relaxed in their situation, Sean wanted to do something fun. He thought maybe going to the beach would fit that idea and allow them to make new memories.

They had just finished breakfast when Sean piped up. "How does the beach sound?"

Jenn looked over at him and smiled. "Sounds great!" She stood from her chair and went into the bathroom. "You remember that weekend we pitched a tent down at Paradise Cove?" She shouted from inside.

"Hell yeah, I remember that. You looked so hot in your bikini. It took everything in me not to jump my best friend." He chuckled.

Jenn opened the bathroom door and looked at him with confusion on her face. "Seriously? Why didn't you say anything?" She stood in front of the sink, toothbrush in her mouth. She seemed to be in shock.

Sean looked at her brushing her teeth and smiled. He remembered everything from that trip. "Say anything? Seriously? You think if I had told you that you had a smokin' bod that we'd have still been friends?" He walked over to the bathroom and leaned in the doorway. "We were teenagers, Jenn. And if I had said anything, do you really think I would have been able to convince you to skinny dip that weekend?" He grinned at her.

Jenn spat in the sink and wiped her mouth on a towel. Looking at him, she smirked. "Nice Sean, just nice." She shook her head and punched his shoulder. "I was thinking more about the bonfires, roasting marshmallows and sunsets we watched. But no, you had to be a perv." She laughed and reached for her hairbrush.

Sean laughed off her little punch. "Yes, I remember all that, too. It was a great weekend. One of many we shared."

"Agreed. I miss that. Us. You and me. The fun we shared. I am just glad my father was lenient with me, so trusting that I was able to go to all the places we went." She sighed, and started brushing her hair.

"We will just have to make some new memories." Sean pushed off the doorway and headed toward his bag. "We'll have to stop and grab some swimwear from a store. I don't seem to have any."

Jenn put her hair up and was ready for the day. "And you think I would have packed something to swim in?" She smirked at him and shook her head.

He looked up at her and smiled. "Well, uh, I guess not. So we'll hit a store for some suits on the way to the beach."

He gave her a full, sexy, breathtaking smile.

Sean grabbed his wallet, and they were off.

With no real beaches in the desert, Sean thought they would spend a few hours over at Mandalay Bay Resort. He wasn't sure if it was open to the public, but it was worth a shot.

Once at the resort, they went directly to registration and asked about a possible day pass for the beach. They were in luck. After purchasing a couple tickets, Sean paid attention to the maps scaled around the place until they found what they had come for. He figured they would be safe there since the beach had a key card access area.

Sean was first to come out of the change room, so he laid out the towels for them to lay on. Taking in the expanse of the beautiful man-made beach, Sean was in awe of the sight before him.

He didn't have to wait long for Jenn to return. Walking toward him was a sight that made his dick twitch. He had seen her naked a few times over the past few days, but he still felt like he had to wipe the drool from his chin. Jenn had a self-esteem issue when they were younger, but the way she carried herself around now, you would never know that. If she could see what he was seeing right now, see how she looked walking in the sexy red-and-white bikini... It showed off every single curve her delicious body had. Self-esteem issues be damned, she would have no complaints. But he supposed most women complained about something about themselves.

He could feel himself getting hard just looking at her. She was so sexy, and she was his. He quickly adjusted himself and sat on a towel.

Jenn walked over to him and looked him over. She smiled and sat on the towel beside him. She reached into her bag, pulled out the sunscreen, and began to apply it to her arms and legs. She glanced over to Sean with a smile and held up the bottle of lotion. "Can you do my back, please?"

Sean tried to stop his erection from busting out of his shorts. The way Jenn was lathering the lotion on her body was one of the sexiest things he had seen, and he thought he was going to blow a nut right there. It took everything not push her on her back and fuck her right there on the beach in front of everyone, children and all. Damn, he had to get his hormones in check; he seemed to be in a sex-crazed daze lately. As much as he loved it, he still needed to be alert. Disguises or not, they were not out of the woods completely.

He knew he was in a daze when he had to ask her to repeat her question. "Sorry, babe, what do you need?" He shook his head slightly and grinned.

"Can you rub this on my back, please?" she asked again, grinning.

He took the bottle from her, shifted his body to sit behind her, and began to apply the lotion.

Jenn moaned as he rubbed. "That feels good."

"Fuck." Sean growled. He quickly finished applying the lotion, handed the bottle back, and stood.

"Are you okay, Sean?" She looked at him biting her lip.

"Just need to cool down." He started toward the water, adjusting himself along the way. When she moaned, he felt a little pre-cum trickle from his penis, and he knew if he didn't cool down soon he was going to blow like a young computer nerd who had just seen his first Playboy centerfold.

***

Jenn watched him walk to the water, and she felt a little bad. She never realized how easily men could be turned on. All she did was moan a little, but hell, it felt great when he was rubbing her back; but at the same time, she felt good knowing she could arouse him.

After soaking up the sun for a few minutes, her mind began to wander back to the conversation she and Sean had back at the hotel. Reminiscing about that trip, a trip she remembered very well, had brought a smile to her face. Seeing Sean in his swimming trunks with his tan abs on display for her eyes to feast on. It was a sight she would never forget. The days were hot and the nights were cool. He always made sure she was warm enough, whether it was with a sweater or by the fire. The walks they had taken along the beautiful beach were long and fulfilling. They were always splashing each other with the cool water as they waded through it, watching the boats go by. Watching the stars at night was common, and chatting by fire light was a favorite. He made her feel like she was the only person who mattered. Spending that first weekend alone with him really flourished her feelings for him.

Clearing her mind of those memories, Jenn thought that a dip in the cool water would be nice and decided to go join him. She sat up, put the lotion in her bag, and began to stand when she got an eerie feeling. A chill ran up her spine. She stood up and looked around, but nothing seemed out of place. She didn't notice anyone looking at her from the surrounding area, so she shook it off and started toward the water.

There were a lot of people in the water, splashing around and laughing, but she had no problem finding Sean. She couldn't miss his glorious body, even if she tried. She had become familiar with it over the past few days and couldn't get enough of it.

She crept up to him as quietly as she could. He was just staring off into space, daydreaming. When she got close enough and remained unnoticed, she pounced. She jumped on his back, trying not to slip, and giggled.

"Are you cool enough?" She wrapped her legs around his waist, her arms around his neck.

Sean reached around and supported her by her ass and gave it a gentle squeeze. "Yeah, I'm cool. The water is very refreshing."

He turned his head to look at her and she smiled, moving her head closer to his. He leaned into her and pressed his damp lips to hers for a slow passionate kiss. He took her bottom lip into his mouth and sucked gently. He bit it once and sucked again, flicking his tongue along the crease, then he plunged in and took the kiss deeper. He pulled back and shifted Jenn around the front of him.

He held her close, cupping her ass.

"Well, I was cool." He slipped his hands under her bikini bottoms and began to caress her ass. He leaned into her again and crushed his lips to hers.

Jenn moaned and shifted her body closer to him. She ran her hands up into his hair. She pulled her face back and bit her lip on a grin, breathing heavy with her chest heaving. "We have to stop, Sean. There are kids around."

Sean squeezed his eyes tight and took a deep breath. "Sorry. You are just so tempting, and it is just so hard to resist you. No matter where we are." He opened his eyes, licked his lips, and smiled. He removed his hands from inside her bikini and set her down. He dipped himself in the water, grabbed her hand and started to head toward the sand.

After a stimulating time in the water and an hour of lying on the beach, Jenn began to feel the same eerie feeling again. She was lying on her stomach, on her towel, beside Sean. She lifted her head and looked around. The fear of the situation they were in had always been sitting in the back of her mind, and being watched once was scary enough. If she was being watched again, it couldn't be a coincidence. She glanced up and down each side of the beach as far as she could see, but it was right in front of her. Fifty yards ahead of her sitting on a picnic table, she noticed a man watching her. She gasped, and a lump formed in her throat, her pulse increasing. It was the same man from the casino. A shiver ran up her spine.

She swallowed and took a few breaths, scrambled to a sitting position, and nudged Sean to wake him. "Sean, wake up."

Sean groaned. "What's the matter, Jenn?" He rolled toward her.

"There was a man, the same man from the casino. He was here. He was watching us." The words rushed out as she was freaking out. This couldn't be a coincidence.

Sean sat up and looked in the direction Jenn was just pointing. "There's no one there."

"But, but…" Jenn looked back, frustrated. She couldn't be losing her mind. She knew she saw him. The man must be playing with her, trying to fuck with her head.

Sean reached over and pulled Jenn into his lap. He kissed the top of her head and held her tight. "I believe you saw someone, babe. But no one's there now. You're safe. I am not going to let anything happen to you." He tipped her head up and planted a quick, firm kiss on her lips.

Jenn got up off his lap and stood. She began to pack up her things. "I have had enough beach time, how about we just walk around and maybe grab something eat." Once packed up, she stood and waited for him.

"Sure, sounds like a plan." He stood and packed up his stuff. Taking hold of her hand, they headed toward the changing rooms.

Back in their street clothes, hand in hand, they walked

along the crowded street, window shopping. They talked comfortably like old times, and laughed with each other like they hadn't missed those years apart. Jenn had begun to get that feeling again while walking, but she just brushed it off. She didn't want Sean thinking she was crazy. She just wanted to enjoy the day.

Jenn was talking, rambling on, as she looked in the windows when her stomach growled. Out of the corner of her eye, she noticed Sean check his watch.

"Let's go eat."

She looked at him and gave his hand a squeeze in acknowledgment. "Sure." They walked toward the next open food venue.

Chapter Fourteen

Simon knew Jake was going to pitter-patter about on the job; it was his brother after all. The only smart thing Jake did was take him on the job. Jake was unaware of Simon's past discretions, and Simon wasn't about to tell him and ruin the fun he planned on having.

Once he and Jake got separate hotel rooms at the dumpy motel at the other end of the strip, Simon told Jake he was going to go catch a hit. Jake seriously thought that Simon was into the drugs, so it benefited him. What Jake didn't know, wouldn't hurt him. Just because he dealt the shit didn't mean he snorted it, too.

Little did Jake know, Simon went to scope out Sean and the girl. He never thought he would luck out so easily when he decided to check out the casino. He stumbled upon them playing slots right at the edge of the playing area. He got himself a drink from the waitress, and he sat at a small table, just watching them. He wanted to see how well they got along, to see if they even realized that they were followed. And to see how well they were taking in the surroundings.

Just as he had figured, Connor's son was a fool. Drinking and playing around without a care in the world, as if his life was not at stake. He knew Connor went soft on his youngest son, allowing him free range during his teenage years. It was too bad his life was going to get cut short. And the girl, man she was beautiful, with a banging body, but she was naïve as shit. He shook his head and sipped his drink.

When Sean left the girl by herself, Simon thought it was his chance to get closer, but thought twice about it. He liked to play games just as much as Connor did.

Maybe the girl wasn't so dumb after all. She seemed to have sensed he was there, because she turned around looking for something. Not once, but twice. On the second time, she noticed him. He just stared at her. He saw no recollection of him in her expression, which was good. He remembered what he did to the girl's mother all those years ago. He didn't have the taste for killing back then. Thinking of the things he could do to her sent thrills up his spine.

He noticed her gathering her things to leave. That was his sign, he had to get out of there before shit hit the fan. He sucked back his drink and immediately left the casino. He had to get back to Jake before he figured something was up.

***

Jake knew it was time to get a little closer to the pair of them, time to put some thoughts into action. He'd never done wrong by his father, and he didn't plan to start now, no matter how hard it was going be to put his own brother into the ground. It had to be done.

Simon had been taking off to places unknown. Jake just figured it was Vegas, and he was sure he was just getting a fix or out getting laid. So he decided to pay no attention to him when it came to comings and goings.

It was midmorning when they began to stake out the

hotel, and it seemed they struck some luck in their timing. They had only been sitting in the café across the way for ten minutes when Jake noticed Sean and Jenn leave the hotel. He didn't notice any necklaces on the woman's neck, just the low cropped tank that presented her blessed breasts to the world. This made him groan. He really needed to get laid soon.

He thought that if she didn't have the pendant on, then they would have to keep a closer eye on them. If he thought about it, he never noticed it on her anytime he saw her, so how were they going to be able to track them? She must have it stashed somewhere, possibly in her purse. It didn't matter to him, as long as they were able to find them wherever they went and he could complete his task and get home.

Jake stood from the table and slapped Simon on the shoulder, getting his attention. "Let's go. They're on the move."

Jake and Simon followed Sean. Keeping up with him wasn't hard, because Jake knew his brother's car well. However, Jake had the advantage as Sean wasn't aware of the vehicle he was in. Once there, Jake didn't want to be seen. He knew Jennifer would recognize him, but she didn't know Simon, so he hid behind a tree while Simon sat on a picnic table to stake out their claim.

"You think he will ever leave her alone?" Jake asked Simon, frustrated that it was taking longer to get their task done than he thought it would.

"Yeah, he'll slip up soon. Your brother is a fool. Look at them, not a care in the world right now. They look like a couple in love." Simon nodded in the Sean's direction.

Jake quickly glanced around the tree to look and puffed out a breath of air. "I just want to get this shit done, man. I want to get home and get laid."

Simon chuckled. "Don't worry, Jake. We will get it done, and you can go home and get your little willy wet." Simon shook his head.

Jake sat and leaned against the tree. He let Simon's jab go and began to think. He never was very close to his brother, but he was still family. He was stuck in a catch-22. His father didn't give a shit about anyone but himself, it was kill or be killed. You fuck with his business, you fucking die. There was no ifs, ands, or buts about it. Life was a game to his father and that was how he was raised. He just wished his father had even a small heart. He knew Sean did everything he could to fit in. He also knew about Jennifer, but he never spoke a word about it. Jake had been called an asshole on more than one occasion. He knew this was what he truly was and always would be. There was no chance for redemption for him, and he knew it. So if his only way of surviving against his father was to kill his brother and his girl, then fuck it, so be it.

"She spotted me." Simon got up from the table and moved behind a tree. Jake scrutinized and waited for clearance. Simon peeked around the tree and sighed.

"'Sup, man?" Jake asked.

"They are on the move again." Simon walked over to Jake and pulled him up from the ground. They began to slowly trail behind them, being careful to stay hidden in the shadows.

Chapter Fifteen

After a fulfilling meal, another hour of laughter and browsing the streets, Jenn and Sean returned to their hotel room. As much as it felt like they were on vacation, they still needed to discuss future plans. Whether they wanted to travel east or south, and decide on names for possible identity changes.

It had been just over a week since they escaped Sean's father, but that didn't mean that they were completely risk-free. Jenn's fear still sat just below the surface. She tried to hide it as much as she could from Sean. She would look over her shoulder when he wasn't looking. He was constantly reassuring her that they were safe, but she knew it would take more than him telling her that to feel it. It needed to be over with for her to feel safe. And as much as she loved being around Sean, Jenn wanted some alone time, too. She wasn't used to being in the presence of a man twenty-four seven.

Finished with her shower, Jenn wrapped a towel around her and began searching for something to wear. While searching she came upon the beautiful necklace she once adored. She scrunched her nose up in confusion and turned to Sean who was lying on the bed watching TV.

"Why is this in here?"

Sean looked over from the TV to her and grimaced. "Uh, yeah, that was on the list of the things Dad had me pick up for you. He said it was a family heirloom or something." He shrugged and continued. "I thought Dad was just being sentimental or some shit. He was always big on things like that."

Jenn huffed. "This is no family heirloom. It was a gift from my ex, Joey. The only nice thing that came from that pathetic excuse of a relationship."

Sean sat up on the bed then moved to the edge. "So, it isn't anything special?"

"No. It is beautiful, but not anything worth taking while being kidnapped or on the run." She bit her lip quizzically, and a chill come over her.

He got off the bed and walked over to her. "What is it, babe?" He wrapped his arms around her and pulled her close. He rubbed his hands up and down her back.

"It's just odd that you were told to bring this, that's all. Did your father have any other plans for me that involved playing dress up?" She looked up into his alluring dark eyes and licked her lips.

Sean groaned and shook his head. "Not that I was told about." He leaned down and gave her a quick kiss on the lips. "But it is a gorgeous piece of jewelry. Maybe we should do the dress-up thing and go out for a fancy dinner." He raised his eyebrows and smirked at her.

"You want to do the fancy thing?" She smiled big at him, pushing aside her recent thoughts to be in the moment with Sean. She hadn't dressed up since her high school prom, which seemed like so long ago.

"Why not? We can go find a boutique and find some dress clothes; shoes and all, and hit up an expensive restaurant and pretend for a night." He smiled big. He slipped one hand in between their bodies and gave the towel a little yank.

She felt the towel give way. She looked into his eyes. They held a sparkle of wickedness. "What are you doing?"

Sean took a small step back and looked Jenn's body up and down. "Gorgeous!" He took the necklace from her and started to put it on her.

Jenn lifted her hair and looked down at the luxury piece and grinned.

Sean tipped her head up and crushed his lips to hers, then stepped back once again. "I want to make love to you wearing only that." He gave her a little peck on the nose, caressed his hands down to hers, and guided her to the bed.

Once at the bed, Sean sat her down. "Move up on the bed, babe. Lay down and allow me to take my fill of your beauty." He stripped himself of his clothing.

Jenn's nerve endings fired with lust as she got comfortable on the bed, naked and waiting. She watched Sean strip his clothes off, and anticipation grew inside her. She didn't think she would get enough of this man and his glorious body.

He climbed onto the bed and advanced slowly. "I am going to kiss, lick, and savor every part of this body." He licked his lips. "I am going to make you squirm and praise my name until you can't speak anymore."

Goose bumps rose on her skin as he spoke. She felt his wet lips on her foot first, then his tongue. She trembled with delight. She could feel herself getting damp just thinking about what all he planned to do to her.

Sean made his way up one leg, kissing, licking, then he repeated the action on the other leg. He worked his way up and up and in.

Two hours later, after an amazing exploit of lovemaking, Jenn got out of bed and dressed. She thought if Sean wanted to do the fancy thing, then he could at least let her go to the boutique herself and pick a dress. It was quite the argument between them. Sean didn't want to take the risk, but Jenn rebutted the fact that he kept telling her they were safe. What was the harm in her going to a few stores alone? of course won and dressed to go shopping for a dress and a pair of shoes.

She walked over to Sean, who sat on the edge of the bed looking frustrated. He really didn't want her to go alone, but Jenn knew she was right. He needed to build up his trust in her, especially since she took care of herself before all these shenanigans.

"Please be careful, Jenn." Sean looked up at her with a grim expression. "Take my phone with you, and if anything happens, you call me here at the hotel." He spoke very firmly.

"I will be okay." She walked over to him, gave him a peck on the lips, and walked toward the door. Looking over her shoulder at him, she spoke. "I won't be long. Shower and relax. I will be back." She smiled and waved before closing the door behind her.

Chapter Sixteen

Dressed in black yoga shorts and a yellow tank with flip-flops, Jenn made her way out of the room, down the elevator, and out into fresh air. Freedom, she thought, what a wonderful feeling. She adjusted the strap of her purse on her shoulder and walked in the direction of the stores. She had promised Sean she wouldn't take long, so she needed to get a move on.

She arrived at a store that looked promising and walked in. The place was full of elegant gowns and dresswear, and she didn't know where to start. Knowing she had limited funds, she headed toward the sales rack first.

She stumbled upon a gorgeous teal, strapless gown. Trying it on, it fit perfectly. Feeling ecstatic about the dress, she had to get undergarments and shoes. She still had the necklace on, the blue and teal combined with her hair color made a wonderful combination.

She couldn't find any shoes she liked in the store, so she paid for what she had and left in search of the perfect pair. She had been walking for only five minutes when she noticed the sign to a store that would have just what she needed and smiled. Holding her bag in hand, she headed toward it. She would have all her shopping done sooner than she thought.

A sudden chill come over her, just like earlier, stopping her in her tracks. She was standing in front of an alleyway, but was unaware of it. She looked around feeling a little off-kilter, but saw nothing. She was just about to continue walking when a gloved hand closed over her mouth, and she was pulled into the alleyway.

***

They had waited all afternoon for Sean and Jenn to come out again. "Simon." He nudged him from reading the paper. "There she is, and she is alone."

Simon looked up and grinned. It was about fucking time. Jake wasn't as stupid as he thought, his brother messed up and the girl was alone. Now was the time to take some action. "Let's follow her. We need to make sure that Sean doesn't come out after her."

"Good idea." Jake grinned and stood from the bench.

The pair of men began to follow Jenn down the street, doing their best to stay hidden.

The girl went into a store and spent less than a half hour inside. Still no Sean to be seen. It was a good sign. Simon turned toward Jake. "You head back and get the car. I am going to catch her off guard just up ahead." He smirked. "No woman can resist shopping with all these stores around, so I'll get the chance to nab her. When you come back with the car, we can take her and move forward with the plans."

Jake reached up and scratched his head. "Yeah, man, I will be back as soon as I can." And he took off.

"What a stupid fucker," Simon mumbled.

When he saw the girl paying for her purchase, he headed down the street and slipped into the alley. He wasn't hiding for long. He was glad for that. He just had to wait for his moment.

He noticed her body stiffen, and she looked around. It was the time. He snuck up behind her and wrapped his gloved hand around her mouth so she wouldn't scream and pulled her into the alley.

***

Jenn tried to scream, but it was muffled by the gloved hand covering her mouth. She attempted to hit and kick the person who held her. Whoever nabbed her knew what he was doing.

She was pulled farther into the alleyway. It was dark and damp smelling. She could feel the tears build in her eyes and begin to fall freely. Suddenly, she was shoved up against a dirty wall. She hit hard enough that it hurt. Hitting her head in the process only made the tears fall harder.

"Oh hush, darling. No need for tears." He narrowed his eyes and an evil grin rose on his face.

Jenn struggled.

"No need to struggle. It will only hurt for a little while." He ran one of his hands up the front of her tank top.

Even with her vision blurry from the tears, she was able to make out the face of the man. It was him. The man from the beach and the casino. She tried to struggle more, to get free from his grasp, with no luck. "Let me go," she mumbled under his hand. She tried her hardest to hold the tears at bay. She wanted to know who the man was and what he wanted. Taking slow, deep breaths, which were limited by his hand and a few sniffs, she tried to settle the tears. Her hands hung freely as he held her against the wall with his body, and pressure against her chest. It was as if the man held no fear of her, like he had no reason to fully subdue her.

"That's better, darling. No more tears." He removed his hand from her mouth. He leaned in and whispered, "Didn't think you'd be caught, hmm?" He pulled back a little, but didn't release her, and smirked.

Jenn thought for a few moments, then she clued in. "You work for Sean's dad?" she whispered. Since she was able, she tried to catch her breath. Even the rapid breathing was enough to calm her.

"Bingo." He looked her up and down. "Did you think a little hair color would change your looks that much? Oh my, what a beautiful necklace." He ran his fingers over it and grinned.

More parts of the puzzle began to sink in. There must be something special about the necklace, which was why Sean was told to bring it. She looked down at the piece of jewelry, trembling slightly. "Y-yes," she stuttered. "My ex gave it to me. Seems too beautiful to part with." She looked up at him again to see his reaction.

"Ah, yes, Joey."

Jenn realized the man knew more than she thought. She had to get away from him, and fast. She attempted to gather all the wits she could and tried to remember the moves she learned in a self-defence class she took. But when you are scared and can't think straight, it is not an easy thing to remember. So she just went with it. The guy was a big guy, but she had to try.

She held her hands at her sides and clenched them. Closing her eyes, she quickly prayed. Now that the man was more lax with her, she may have a chance. So, she took it. "Joey was an asshole," she spat out. She took a deep breath, lifted her foot, and stomped down on his foot. "And so are you." She yelled. She swung her hand that didn't hold the bags and punched the guy in the jaw. Once she felt him release her, she ran. She never looked back to see if she was being followed. She just held onto her bag and ran as fast as the adrenaline in her body would take her. Back to the hotel, back to Sean. They needed to find out what the significance of the necklace was and make a run for it.

Chapter Seventeen

The door whipped open to the room making Sean jump up off the bed. Taking in a ruffled Jenn, he rushed over to her. "Babe, what's wrong?"

Jenn dropped her bag and purse and ran right into Sean's arms. She was breathing heavily and sobbing uncontrollably. She gripped this shirt tight and tried to take slower breaths. She was shaking so much Sean knew something scared her. He knew he shouldn't have let her go on her own. He began to rub his hands up and down her back, trying to settle her rattled nerves. "Jenn." He kissed the top of her head, letting her know that she was safe, that she could talk to him. He could feel her body begin to relax a little as the time passed, and he led her to the bed to sit down. "Talk to me, Jenn. What happened?"

Jenn sat on the bed as directed. He noticed her sobbing, breathing, and shaking were starting to settle. She wiped the tears from her cheeks and looked up at him. "The man I told you I saw watching, remember?" She shivered.

He turned his body to be closer to her and took her hands in his. "You mentioned that you saw someone watching." How could Sean have been so stupid, letting that tidbit of information go. If he had listened, he would have paid closer attention; and wouldn't have ignored that weird note.

She nodded her head. "Yes, twice. And when I was shopping, he grabbed me and pulled me into an alleyway." She took a deep breath, and Sean knew that this was bad news. It had to be one of his father's men. They had been followed and he let them get to her.

Sean immediately stood from the bed, releasing her hands in the process. He raked his hands through his hair in frustration. He began to pace the floor in front of her. "Someone fucking grabbed you?" he shouted. He instantly turned to her and looked her up and down, checking for signs of injury. "Are you hurt?" He clenched his fists at the base of his neck. "Fuck, I shouldn't have let you out of here alone. I fucking knew it." He stomped toward the closest wall and punched it in anger.

Jenn jumped from the bed and ran to him. "Sean, I am okay. I got away." She pulled him into a hug. Tears continued streaming down her cheeks.

He grabbed onto her shirt and held her tight. He couldn't believe the mess they had gotten themselves into. He tucked his head into the crook of her neck and stood there. He willed his anger to subside, knowing she was okay. There were no physical marks on her that he could see, so he needed to pull himself together and help her through this. He was supposed to be the strong one, her protector. He breathed in her scent, the vanilla lotion he loved, and relaxed as much as he could. The lotion would always remind him of better days.

"Jenn, if this man is one of my father's, that means he's very dangerous." He looked up into her damp eyes. He leaned back just enough to bring his arms up and wipe away the tears. "You were very lucky to have gotten away. He could have killed you on the spot." Full of fear he pleaded with her; he wanted to make her understand the seriousness of it all. "I am sorry for getting angry, but I don't think you really understand what we are dealing with."

She sniffed and looked into his eyes. She must have realized the truth because her whole body began to tremble.

"It's okay. I am sorry. I won't go out without you anymore. He knew who I was with this pathetic disguise. How stupid could we be, thinking they would work?" She swallowed hard. "Deem me educated in your words. I shall stay here with you for my own safety." She stepped back from him and walked to the bathroom. She took a quick drink from the cup on the counter and returned to the bed and sat down.

Sean paced the room once again, trying to gather his thoughts.

"Sean?" she called to him. "Sean!"

Sean stopped in his tracks and looked at her. "Yeah, babe?"

Jenn sighed and raised her eyebrows. "If you don't sit down soon, you will wear a hole in the floor." She smiled at him.

He gave her a slow grin. "You are a funny girl, aren't you?"

She shrugged and smiled at him. She patted the spot beside her. "Have a seat. Tell me what is on your mind."

He sat beside her and took a deep breath. "For starters, can you describe the guy? If I have a description of him, maybe I can figure out who it is, and then I will have a better idea of what we're in for." He looked over at her with hope of at least that little bit of knowledge.

Jenn sat up straight and swallowed. "Yes, I can

describe him." She licked her lips and continued. "He was tall, built like a fucking bull and had short dark hair."

"That's all?" Sean asked, raising his eyebrows in curiosity.

"No." She took a deep breath and quirked her lips. "He had brown eyes and just below his right eye, he had this scar."

Sean perked up, getting a feeling he knew who the man was. He just had one question to ask to confirm it. "What did the scar look like?" He held his breath anticipating her answer.

She bit her lip and scrunched her eyebrows. A thoughtful look settled upon her. "It was somewhat circular, it didn't look like your normal type of scar, more of a burn scar."

Sean fell back on the back and thumped his fists on the mattress. Puffing out breaths in anger and fear. "Simon. He sent fucking Simon." He tipped his head to the side to look toward her. "Simon is the type to shoot first and ask questions later. Fuck me, we need to make a plan to get out of here, and fast."

Jenn touched her throat, touched the necklace. Looking down at him she asked. "Sean?" She reached over and touched his arm to get his attention since his eyes were closed.

He opened his eyes and looked up to her. "Yeah?"

She fingered the necklace once more. "This guy, Simon, he was interested in my necklace. Why would that be?" She reached back to undo the clasp.

Sean sat up and helped take the necklace off. "He was interested in the necklace?" He repeated her question, wondering what possibly could be so interesting about the beautiful piece of jewelry.

"Yes, and he knew about my ex, Joey." Once the necklace was off, she handed it to him

"Like I said before, you were watched, and not just by me." He looked down at the necklace in his hand and turned it about, looking to see if there was anything out of the ordinary.

"Well shit, that could mean that Joey works for your dad?" She tucked her legs under her and watched him intently as he assessed the jewelry.

"No, there is no Joey on his payroll that I am aware of. He may have paid him to do something on the side, but he is not an actual employee per se." He turned his body just slightly to get the light from the windows to shine on the pendant in his hands, and then he saw it. At just the right angle he could see the dark little chip inside. "Well fuck, there is a goddamn tracker in this." He jumped up from the bed and quickly stomped on the necklace, making sure to crush the sparkling blue jewel. He bent down and sifted through the tiny pieces and found the tracker and growled. He picked it up and went into the bathroom. He lifted the lid to the toilet, dropped the tracker in, and flushed.

Sean came out of the bathroom and noticed the regret in her eyes. She must think it was her fault. "This is not your fault, babe." He crouched in front of her and grabbed her hands. He looked up into her eyes and smiled. "My father is an evil, vindictive man, and he sees no wrong in his doings. Right now we need to figure out if Simon is alone and see why he seems to be fucking with our heads."

"Okay."

He nodded and pulled her into a hug.

Chapter Eighteen

When all the anger had subsided and emotions had stabilized, they decided to order some room service and stay in for the rest of the day. Sean had told Jenn that he felt that since Simon failed in his attempt to nab her, it was best to stay indoors. They needed to change hotels since the tracker now permanently said where they were. If they move places, they might be a bit safer.

Not knowing where Simon was, or who else was watching them, Jenn and Sean packed up and attempted to blend in the crowd to sneak out of the Fremont. They needed a new place to stay, but wanted to stay close to where the car was parked for an easy escape.

The closest place was the D Hotel. While still watching for onlookers, Jenn pulled Sean inside. They begged and pleaded with the concierge to check in under an unknown name, quickly giving their reasons and promising them no trouble. Neither of them could believe it worked. A small suite was offered for cash upfront, so they paid and the deal was made.

After a restless sleep, Jenn woke midmorning to a gorgeous sight. Lying beside her was her best friend, her protector and now lover. The blanket laid low on his body revealing a gloriously naked chest, one that she was very tempted to touch. She peeked up at his face to ensure that he was sleeping. His eyes were closed, and his face was relaxed. She listened to his breathing, which was steady and slow. He was indeed sleeping. That made her smile. It was a rare thing to see as of late, a relaxed Sean, and she just took in the sight for a few moments. As she glanced further, she noticed the bulge in the sheets, and she grinned. She knew it was probably not a good time to be playing around, but she needed a distraction. The beautiful sight before her could definitely distract her.

Trying not to wake him, Jenn quickly slipped her tank and boxers off and tossed them onto the floor. She lazily turned onto her side and began caressing Sean's naked chest with her hand in slow, soft circles from around his nipples down to his navel and back up. The little hairs on his body rose, and she heard him moan. She bit her lip and stopped. She looked up to see if she woke him. His eyes were still closed and his breathing remained steady. It appeared she had not. She looked down at the bulge and it appeared to be bigger. A grin formed on her face.

She moved her hand down to his waist and started again. Gently, she eased her finger back and forth across the skin, from hip to hip and up to his navel and back to his waist and repeated. She earned the same response as a few moments ago. His eyes were still closed. Feeling a bit braver, she slowly moved her hand under the sheet and began to caress down his inner groin area, very close to his erection, which twitched the closer she got. Her nipples hardened and dampness formed between her legs. She was getting sexually aroused the more she touched him, and when his penis twitched, she had to swallow a moan of her own.

He shifted his head on the pillow to look toward her.

"Babe?" He grinned.

Jenn looked up at him, noting that his eyes were open. She gave him a shy smile. "Yes?"

"What are you doing?"

She licked her lips. "Exploring." She stroked his erection once. "Would you like me to stop?" She tipped her head down, suddenly shy, but didn't remove her hand from his massive erection. She loved the feel of it, the skin soft and smooth, and his size... She loved the size. She didn't have anyone else to compare it with really, besides Joey, but Sean was perfect to her.

He reached his arm over and tipped her head up to look at him with his finger. "Hey now, no being shy with me. Not now, not ever. Never again, babe. It's you and me against the world, with or without clothing." He winked at her.

He wrapped his hand around hers, which was still on his erection, and stroked.

Jenn took the hint and moved her hand along with his. She watched Sean's facial expression the whole time. Knowing the pleasure he was receiving was because of her made her feel ten feet tall. She loved that she was able to do that for him. She glanced down at what their hands were doing and smiled as she looked back up at him. Just as she looked up, his moist lips gently touched hers, and her body began to tingle.

Sean removed his hand from over hers, setting it on her hip. He slid it up her hip bone to the outer side of her breast and back down.

Jenn shivered at his caress.

He shifted his upper body and turned toward her, pressing his lips tight to her.

His lips were warm, soft and welcoming. She loved

having them on her.

He licked the seam of her lips, and he slipped his tongue in. They both groaned. His hand stopped on her hip, and he pulled her close.

When Sean pulled her closer, she lost her grip on him. She moved her hand up to his chest and moved a leg over his while continuing to kiss him. Taking in all that he was giving. While moving her leg over, she grazed his erection. She felt his groan in her mouth as they kissed.

She didn't want to end up in an awkward position so she pulled back from the kiss and straddled him.

Sean cupped her ass, assisting in the movement. Lust flew through her.

He squeezed her cheeks and began to caress her. He ran his finger in the lower dips of her spine down to her upper thighs.

Jenn shivered, feeling dampness between her legs as she sat upon him, his erection just barely touching her mound. All she had to do was shift her hips a bit and she would feel him. She would get all of him. A little tingle in her chest came upon her. She had never been in charge when it came to intimacy. She didn't want to ruin things by going too fast, but with the look on Sean's face, the size of his cock and all the lust flowing through her, she wasn't able to slow down. She placed her hands on his masculine chest and leaned forward just enough to slide her wet pussy along his cock. The feeling of him hitting her clit sent jolts of pleasure up through her, and she moaned. She licked her lips and swallowed. Leaning down and taking Sean's lips with hers, the pleasure took control of her. She continued to rub herself on him while teasing Sean with her mouth. Her tongue wrestling with his, moans and groans were the only sounds present.

Sean eased back. "Jenn. If you don't stop, I am going to fucking blow before I even get inside you." He growled, kissing her lips, the corner of her mouth, her neck.

"It just feels so damn good." She panted.

He gripped her hips and shifted her. "I know what will feel so much better, babe." He thrust hard and deep. "Fuck, you feel amazing. Jenn. I never want to leave your warmth." He thrust again, and again, gaining a steady pace. "This is fucking home. My fucking home. No matter where we are, you are my home." He leaned up and took her lips, slipping his tongue in and teasing hers.

Jenn gave up the little control she thought she had and let Sean take her on the ride of pure bliss. Zing after zing of pleasure struck her as he pumped into her hard and long. His kisses took her further into the lustful haze she was in. She could feel her toes curl. She began to move her hips to stay in rhythm with him and grind her clit into his pelvis when they hit. She didn't know how long she would last. She was in a pleasure overload, and she loved it.

She released herself from the kiss and leaned up. She continued to raise and lower herself down onto him. Hands on his chest to hold her up, breath rapid, heart rate increasing. So much pleasure. She didn't want it to end, but she was getting that tingly feeling in her stomach, and her muscles felt funny. She knew it was coming fast. "I'm close," she moaned.

Sean reached up, cupped her breasts, and rubbed her nipples. "You can come, babe." His movements became jittery, and after two quick hard thrusts he yelled out, "I love you."

Her pussy clenched around him and got wetter as she screamed out his name. She collapsed on top of him, breathing heavy. He wrapped his arms around her midsection and kissed her deeply. Rolling onto their sides, he slid his penis out of her, and pulled the blanket up over them. He pulled her to him and wrapped his arms around her as they fell into a peaceful sleep.

Chapter Nineteen

Jenn woke suddenly in a cold sweat and screamed. The nightmare had invaded her sleep again, but worse. She was able to put a name to the eyes and voice in her dreams. Tears streamed down her cheeks, her breath rapid and mouth dry. The dream was so vivid and clear she couldn't believe she didn't realize it when she first noticed him.

"Babe?" Sean spoke sleepily. "Are you okay? You are shaking. Oh shit, you're crying. What's wrong?" Sean turned over and sat up. He wrapped his arm around her shoulder and pulled her closer to him. He ran his fingers through her hair and waited.

Jenn tucked her head into Sean's warm, naked chest and accepted his comfort. She needed a minute to control her thoughts and her breathing. When she was able, she pulled back and looked up at him. "Simon killed my mother."

Sean growled, "Are you sure?"

She nodded as a lonely tear escaped from her eye.

Sean took a deep breath. "Fuck." His fists clenched behind her, and he pulled her tight.

Jenn began to tremble again. Knowing Sean was upset about the situation meant that things were worse than she thought. They were in deep. She was entitled to take a few minutes to freak out. But after that, she needed to help Sean figure a way out of the shit. She wondered if calling her father would help. Not really having thought of him beforehand, she supposed better late than never.

"Sean, what if I called my father?" she mumbled into his chest.

He eased her back and lifted her chin up to look at her. "What was that, Jenn?"

"I asked, what if I called my father, would that help any?" She tipped her head a bit and scrunched her nose in curiosity.

Sean leaned back and grabbed the back of his neck. He blew out a long breath. "I'm not sure. You could try, but you need to remember, it's because of your father that you ended up in this mess in the first place."

With a look of defeat, she looked down to her lap. "I know, but if he has any information, or if there is anything he could do, it's worth a shot, right?" Always the one to never give up hope without trying first, Jenn would try anything before giving up.

Sean grabbed his phone off the bedside table and slid his thumb over the screen. It was only four a.m. He turned back. "It's still really early. Why don't we shower, grab a bite to eat, and then you can call him if you still feel like it." He smiled at her, pulled her in for a hug, and kissed her forehead.

"Okay."

After a blissful shower, where Sean took Jenn up against the shower wall, then proceeded to wash every inch of her body, they ordered breakfast and sat out on the balcony to watch the sun rise.

Jenn had never taken the time to actually take in the

beauty of the sunrise. What a sight to behold. The colors were beautiful. It reminded her of happier days when she was young and she had Sean by her side and was oblivious to all the bullshit going on. She turned to him and just stared. He was everything she remembered and so much more. The boy he used to be had turned into a gorgeous man. She still hurt from his sudden disappearance, but what was a few years of angry drought when she could have a future full of happiness?

He turned to look at her and raised his eyebrows in question. "Babe?"

Jenn bit her lip and just kept staring at him.

Sean chuckled. "Jenn, seriously, why are you staring? Do I have something on my face?" He reached up and ran his hand over his mouth.

Jenn giggled. "No, you have nothing there, silly."

"Well, what is it?" He turned in his chair to face her.

Jenn felt her face getting hot in embarrassment. She looked down in her lap and tried to move away. "Nothing," she mumbled.

Sean caught her before she was able to move. He grabbed her hands in his and looked down at her. "Jennifer Samos, look at me."

She looked up at him. He was gorgeous. His eyes were shining brightly at her, lovingly, eager to hear what she had to say. She didn't know why she had become shy all of a sudden. There was just something about him that took her breath away.

Sean pleaded with his eyes and smiled. "Well…?"

She blew out the breath she hadn't realized she had been holding. "I was staring because you are hot." She ran her teeth along her bottom lip and began to chew on her inner cheek.

"You think I'm hot, babe?" Sean grinned.

"Yes," she simply replied.

"You think I'm hot." He wiggled his eyebrows and grinned.

Jenn couldn't help but laugh. "Yes, I think you are fucking hot, okay." She almost yelled at him while laughing. She was about to stand from her chair when Sean pulled her closer, bringing her to straddle him.

He looked into her eyes and licked his lips. "I think you're hot, too." He smiled, leaning into her and gave her kiss on the lips. "I want you to be able to tell me everything you are thinking, feeling, or even wonder, Jenn. We are in this together."

"I know."

"My biggest regrets in life are letting my father control me and leaving you." He kissed her forehead and looked back into her eyes. "These are two things I want to make up for. I am not going to let my father control me anymore, and you are my life now. You were mine when we were kids, but I was stupid then, ruining things. I will do everything in my power to make up for that mistake."

"I never knew why you ran from me. You didn't really explain it to me. You just said it was too dangerous. Why didn't you just trust me, Sean?" She wanted answers for the past, even a little bit of one would help her move on from it.

Sean adjusted Jenn in his lap and wrapped his arms around her. "I did trust you. I didn't trust my father. The night I left you… That night I knew you were going to tell me your feelings. I noticed all the little things between us, especially your feelings. I felt them too. But that was the night I let my father's control go too far." He swallowed hard. "I killed my first hit that night, right before I met with you. And if my father had that much control over me, I knew it was too dangerous to have you around. I told him no so many times about being part of his family business, but he didn't accept that answer. He chose that night to cement my future. I had to break ties with you, no matter how much it hurt us both." He blew out a breath.

Tears began to run down her cheeks, and she swallowed the lump forming in her throat. "You killed a man?" she whispered.

"I didn't have a choice really. But yeah, I did. I'm not proud to say that, nor am I proud to say he wasn't my last either. But I will say, I am not planning to kill again, unless it is to protect you." He brought his arms around and wiped the tears from her face with his fingers.

She nodded her head in understanding. She knew, or at least understood, that Sean was not the kind of man to do something for nothing. He was being controlled by his father, the rat bastard that he was. So if his father was that bad, did that mean her father was just as bad?

"I am not proud of the man I was, Jenn. But I'm not that man anymore. And if you let me, I promise to be the man you deserve." He tipped her head up and looked into her eyes and gave a small smile.

She reached her arms up and wrapped them around his neck. She pressed her lips to his and gave him a quick kiss. Leaning back, she smiled. "I understand. I just needed that little bit of closure. I believe you did it to protect me, and I know you will protect me now. But what I need to do now is call my dad and find out what the hell he did that put my life on the line." She let go of him, wiggled her butt back on his lap, and stood up. She reached her hand out to him and he took it and walked with her into the room.

Chapter Twenty

Jenn sat on the side of the bed and picked up the hotel phone. Taking a deep breath, she looked at Sean and hoped she was making the right decision. She dialed her father's number and waited. The phone rang three times before she heard his deep voice.

"Hello?"

"Daddy." Jenn spoke softly. Here was the man she had loved and thought was innocent her whole life, but now knew differently. She cleared her throat.

"Jennifer. Baby girl, is that you?" His voice stuttered. It sounded as if he was going to cry.

Jenn knew that voice, she had heard it once before when her mother had died.

"Yes, Daddy, it's me."

"Where are you, baby girl?" he asked.

"I'm safe."

"But where, Jennifer?" His voice got louder, sounding concerned.

"What did you do, Daddy?" Jenn wanted answers. She knew her father was probably upset and concerned, but she didn't really trust him anymore.

"What do you mean?"

She could hear the suspicion in his voice. Knowing her

father just went from her pet name, to her full name, showed he knew exactly what she was talking about. She wasn't his naïve little girl anymore. She gripped the phone tightly. "I think you know, Dad," she spat. "Tell me why there's a hired hit on me."

There was silence on the other end. She knew she struck a nerve; she had him. If he didn't answer her honestly, she would never speak to him again. She would wipe her hands of him. She would never forgive him for everything that had come to past.

"Well…I am waiting," she gritted out.

She heard him sigh. "I'm sorry, baby girl, I fucked up."

"You fucked up?" she screeched. "You more than fucked up, Daddy. I don't know exactly what you did or why, but whatever it was I will never forgive you for it. I now know that your shit cost Mom her life, and now it may cost me mine." She growled. "You need to fucking fix this. How could you do this to us? Don't you love me? Didn't you love mom?"

She heard a crash on the other end of the phone. It was as if he was breaking things while talking to her. "Yes, I fucking loved your mother, and I love you, too." He was breathing heavy. "I made a big mistake back then, and I've paid for it ever since. Fuck." She heard another crash.

"Well, what the fuck happened now? Why are there men after me? For fuck's sake, Dad, did you not learn the first time?" Her body began to shake in anger, her emotions getting the best of her. Fear, anger, hate, everything was building up while talking to the man she once looked up to, only to find out it was all lies.

"I was trying to fucking protect you, to protect my business." His voice seemed defeated. All his anger seemed to be gone, the fight in his voice, vanished. "Connor always tried to ruin things for me, so I tried to ruin him back." He sighed.

She looked up at Sean. "So, you are trying to say this is Mr. Green's fault?"

Sean cocked his eyebrows and tilted his head.

"Yes. Jennifer, my business is not all that legal," he answered. "And neither is Connor's. I won't get into details. But to make a long story short, he turned a few of my men against me to go work for him. So, I disrupted one of his shipments, and one of his men were killed by accident." She heard him blow out a breath.

Jenn brought a hand to her head and closed her eyes to try and stop the tears. "You're telling me I have some crazy people after me because of your fight with Mr. Green? Over drugs? It is drugs, right?" She opened her eyes and took a breath. She couldn't believe the petty bullshit coming from him.

"I'm sorry, baby girl. I really am. But, yes."

Jenn couldn't believe her ears. He actually admitted it. He came clean to his sins of the past and present. He was a horrible man—a selfish, horrible man. "I can't believe this. You were my world. The only parent I had left. But now, I am sorry to say, you're nothing. You got mom killed, and the same man who killed her is after me. You obviously aren't man enough to fix it, so good-bye, Dad." She hung up on him, setting the phone down in its cradle and let the tears fall.

Sean pulled her into a hug, wrapping his arms around her.

"I hate him so much," she cried out.

"Shh, it's okay. I've got you." He held her head to his chest and rubbed her back.

She looked up at Sean and wiped her face. "We sure

struck gold in the parent gene pool." She laughed.

Sean grinned and shook his head. "Yeah, they sure are fucked up, aren't they?"

"If or when I become a mom, I don't ever want to be like our fathers."

"You would make a wonderful mom, Jenn." He leaned in and kissed the side of her mouth, then the other side, pressing his lips to her's. "Your mom was amazing. I am sure you will take after her."

She slapped his shoulder playfully. "You are going to make me cry again, and I don't think I have any more tears left in me."

"I'm only being truthful."

After few deep breaths to gain composure, Jenn sat up straight. "Okay, so what now?"

Sean gave her a teasing smirk. "Well, we could, you know…" He wiggled his eyebrows.

Jenn laughed. "You are becoming a fucking horn dog, Sean."

"Only with you, babe."

"Well, no!"

Sean chuckled and shrug his shoulders. "Okay, well what would you like to do?"

"Hmm, well Simon knows we're in Vegas, but doesn't know about the hotel change. I don't want to hide in here all the time." She pouted. "How about we see what this hotel has to offer, show ourselves out in the open, and have lunch."

Sean sighed and narrowed his eyes. "Okay, but you need to stay close. I don't trust Simon, but for you, I would do anything. And if I go to the bathroom, you come with me." He grinned wickedly. "Simon found us once, we can only pray he doesn't find us again."

They had been at the little casino the new hotel had for an hour, and no signs of Simon. Jenn was still upset, but was beginning to relax a little knowing that Sean was beside her and wouldn't let anything happen to her. She kept her eyes peeled and her fear below the surface. Simon may be out for blood, but she wasn't going down without a fight.

After an hour at the slots, she was breaking even. Her mind kept going back to her dream and to Simon and the whole situation as she played. She wasn't having the fun she thought she would, but at least she was out of the room. The slots were such a mindless game, just having to insert the coins and pull the lever. She was in her own little world; she didn't hear Sean calling her name.

"Jenn!" Sean called and lightly shook her shoulder.

Jenn was brought out of her daze when she felt her body being shaken. Suddenly all the noise and lights were apparent to her again. She heard Sean's voice and looked at him. "Sorry, was thinking about things."

"That was some deep thought." He chuckled.

She grinned at him. "Yeah, sorry." She finally noticed the alarms going off on his machine and looked at it, then him again. "You won?"

"Yeah, babe, I did."

"That's awesome, how much?"

"Five thousand, I think." He winked at her and smiled.

Jenn got excited. She jumped up off her stool and gave him a hug. "Holy shit, that rocks."

People all around the area were beginning to look in their direction to see what the commotion was about. Members of the casino began to approach them to validate the win and to escort them to the cashier for their winnings.

Chapter Twenty-One

After cashing in, they took a walk to the nearest pizza place and grabbed a large one to bring back to the room. Sean thought it was best to stay indoors. He wanted to try and plan out his next steps for keeping Jenn safe.

Back in the room, Sean set the food on the table, grabbed a few bottled waters from the mini-fridge and turned some music on with the phone. He kicked his shoes off and sat in a chair across from Jenn at the table. He handed her a bottle of water and opened the delicious-smelling pizza, taking a slice.

Sitting at the table in the room, enjoying a slice of hot pepperoni pizza, Jenn looked like she was in a world of her own again. Sean hoped she would fill him in on her thoughts soon.

She swallowed her bite of food and looked up at Sean. "Sean, I've been thinking."

Thankful for the interruption and that she was finally going to open up, he finished his bite and set down his slice of pizza. He wiped his mouth with a napkin and looked up at her. "Okay, and what were you thinking?"

"Well, you remember how I used to do those crossword puzzles when I was younger?"

He narrowed his eyebrows in curiosity. "Yeah, why?"

"Well, when you disappeared on me, I got more into puzzles and such." She licked her lips and swallowed.

Sean leaned forward and set his arms on the table, intrigued to hear what she was going to say.

"Well, I've been thinking about this whole situation and how you said I had to remember something. But I don't think I am thinking along the same lines as you." She scrunched her nose up and bite her lip.

"What do you mean, Jenn? What I needed you to remember was your mother's death. Sorry to be blunt, but that was how I took it from my father. When he presented the file, he was blaming your father." Sean was getting himself confused trying to explain himself. He sat back in his chair and began to rub his neck. "Well shit, I don't even know anymore. I am sorry, Jenn, I have been schooled by my father on what to say in situations for so long." He blew out a long deep breath.

Jenn looked at him intently, took a deep breath, and sat up straight in her chair. "Do you want your father to pay for what he has done to you?"

Sean looked at her, still confused. He didn't understand what she meant. "Pay?"

"Yes, pay for his control over you, your life, your actions, for his actions." She tilted her head.

He leaned forward in his chair, curious to what she was thinking. "What do you mean, Jenn? How does he 'pay' for that?"

She smiled big. "Well, as I said, I like to do puzzles. I have been trying to piece this together in my mind." She abruptly stood up, went over to the nightstand and opened the drawer. She took out a pad of hotel paper and a pencil and brought it back over to the table. She began to write a few things down.

Sean leaned over to see what she was writing. He saw a list form -

Hired a hit man to murder mother

Setup boyfriend to seduce and gift a tracker

Arranged kidnapping and ransom

Possible hire hit for murder of me and his own son

When Sean noticed the boyfriend part he looked up at her. "Can that be listed? I mean, can that really be used?"

"I will use anything and everything against him." She looked up at him with a determined look in her eyes. Sean kept his mouth shut and waited.

"Okay, fair enough. So, explain this to me."

Jenn set the pencil down and began. "Well, the memory that I remember, thanks to you, is Simon. Simon killed my mother."

"Okay." He shifted himself in the chair. He tried to think about where she was headed.

"Well, Simon works for your dad." She raised her eyebrows.

"Yeah." He was sort of getting where she was going, but still didn't see how that was going to work.

She shook her head and took a deep breath. "Sean, for fuck's sake. I or we could take your father's whole damn business down. He killed, or rather, had my mother killed. He had me kidnapped. He wants me dead because I know, I fucking know, he set it all up. Don't you see this?" Her voice was getting louder with every word she spoke.

It was like a bright lightbulb turned on in the darkest of rooms. Now that made sense. The whole situation was pieced together. Of course she knew about it. Why else would his father want her dead. Damn, why was he so blind to that piece of information from the get-go. He instantly reached for her hand and smiled. "Tell me the fuck how we do it." As much as he hated to do it to his family, he knew it was the only way to get out from under his father. His brothers be damned. They didn't give a shit about him, never did. The only thing that meant anything to him was sitting in front of him.

She grabbed his outreached hands and smiled. "First, we are packing up and going home. If we are fighting back, we are doing it there. He may think he will have the advantage against us, but I don't plan on giving up or dying anytime soon."

Sean had never felt so proud of this woman in his life. He could see the emotional walls crumbling down and a whole new fight build up inside of her. He had been the one protecting her growing up. Never once had he seen her stand up for herself. But now, seeing the light shine in her eyes, the determination of not backing down, he got a tingly feeling in his chest. He was proud and truly loved this woman.

He got up from his chair, rushed around the table, and picked Jenn up off of hers. He tossed her over his shoulder and smacked her ass. He adjusted his erection—he got hard just thinking of the things was going to do to her before they left the hotel.

Jenn squealed. She grabbed the waist of his pants and held on as he carried her over to the bed. "Sean, what are you doing?" She laughed.

"I am going to enjoy my woman before we have to sit in the car for hours." He tossed her onto the bed and wiggled his eyebrows at her. He reached down to the hem of his shirt and pulled it up and over his head. He tossed it on the floor and grinned at her.

She licked, then bit her lip and sat up. She mimicked

his actions and removed her shirt as well. She immediately began to undo her pants, stripping them off and tossing them on the floor.

Watching her strip her pants away and sit on the bed in only a sexy, red bra and panties, Sean's patience ran thin. He was quick to remove his jeans and boxers. His rock-hard erection pointed where it wanted to go. He stroked it twice just to tease her and crawled onto the bed. He moved overtop of Jenn and took her lips with a deep-seated passion, giving her everything he had and wasn't going to stop until they were both satiated and unable to move.

Chapter Twenty-Two

After a shower and packing, they checked out of the hotel and loaded up the car. Neither of them looked forward to the drive, or what they planned to do when they got home, but they knew it would be worth it.

Sean pulled up to the nearest coffee shop and ran in. He returned with a couple of coffees.

Jenn made herself comfortable in the passenger seat. She offered to take a turn driving, but he declined. It was only about a four-hour drive, maybe a little more, so it wouldn't be too bad. She turned the radio on and sipped her coffee. She was excited to be heading home, but also afraid of what could happen if things didn't work out as planned. She had to think positive. She glanced at Sean while he drove them out of the city, and smiled. She really hoped everything worked out in the end and they could finally be happy and that Sean could feel free with having his father out of his life.

Sean looked over to her and returned the smile. He reached a hand over the console and took hold of hers and gave it a squeeze. "I love you, Jenn," he stated simply and returned his eyes to the road.

"I love you, too." Jenn looked out the windshield and

her thoughts began to wander again. She wanted to make sure she had everything planned out to ensure that Sean was free and clear from the law at the end of the situation. She explained as much as she could to him after their sex marathon. He seemed to understand his part in the fight, and she hoped it didn't backfire.

They were about an hour and half into the drive when Jenn got the creepy tingle she got when she was being watched or followed. She didn't want to mention anything to Sean, so she just looked in the side mirror. There was a car behind them. She didn't recognize it, but then again, it was a highway, and it could have been anyone. She was going to let it slide, but when the other cars were passing them in the passing lane but that car remained behind them, she began to get a little creeped out.

"How much longer till we're home?"

Sean glanced at her in the darkness and back to the dark road ahead of him. "A few more hours, why?"

"Well, don't change what you are doing, but we are being followed." She remained sitting as she was in her seat, trying to act casual. Casual was not an easy feat, especially when her pulse started to accelerate.

Sean glanced in his mirrors. "Are you sure?"

"Yep. That car has been behind us for a while, while other cars have been passing us."

Sean blew out a breath. "Fuck."

Jenn turned her head and looked at him. "What?"

"It's Jake. It has to be him. He's the one who's with Simon. I should have known."

"How do you know?" She looked at him curiously.

"We don't have the tracker anymore, so how else would Simon know what car to follow?"

"What do you mean, Sean?"

"Simon doesn't know my car, Jenn. It's not often that I see him. He was always called in when I wasn't around. My brothers know him more than I do. But Jake knows my car." He slammed his fist on the steering wheel.

Jenn narrowed her eyes in thought. "Jake is your brother. The brother that was at the house?"

"Yes, the fucker that hurt you." He growled again. He quickly looked at her. "I feel stupid for not realizing that he would be there, too." He looked back at the road.

"You can't know everything, Sean. Try and relax. We are going home, and we are going to fix this." She reached for his hand and squeezed it in reassurance. She hoped he didn't feel how clammy her hand was. She didn't want him to realize just how scared she was.

Taking a few deep breaths, he nodded.

Jenn got comfortable again in her seat, kept hold of Sean's hand, and waited out the rest of the ride home. She did everything she could to keep her mind settled, to calm her racing pulse and keep her breathing steady. She hoped that nothing bad would happen on the drive. The last thing she wanted was to be in a car accident, but she supposed worse things could happen.

A few hours later, they arrived at Jenn's place. It was the early hours of the morning. Nothing exciting happened on the drive. Simon and Jake remained behind them the whole way and even followed them to Jenn's. They speed off when Sean pulled into her driveway.

It had been a long drive; they were both exhausted and were in need of sleep. Sean retrieved the bags from the trunk as she requested, while Jenn unlocked the door to her house. She stepped inside and flicked on a light, and Sean followed behind. He set the bags down by the door and stretched.

"Home sweet home." Jenn turned to him and smiled.

"You have a great place, babe." He pulled her into a hug and gave her a peck on the lips.

"Thanks." She yawned. "Now, let's try and get some sleep before the shitstorm starts." She went and locked the door, put the chain on, and took hold of Sean's hand. Together they walked to her bedroom.

Both were beyond exhausted and hoped that they could get an hour or two of sleep at least before trouble came. Neither were sure what kind of fight they had in them at the moment. Stripping down to almost nothing, they crawled under the blankets of her bed, cuddled up, and fell right to sleep.

Connor was sitting in his den sipping on a glass of dark amber whiskey when Jake and Simon walked into the room. Connor looked at them with a sneer on his face. "What the fuck is Simon doing with you, son?"

Jake walked up to the bar and poured himself a drink. He went and sat in the chair across from his father. "I took him with me. I thought I could get the job done faster with him there." He sipped the dark liquid, feeling it burn when he swallowed. He needed the shot because when he told his father the job was not done, there was going to be hell to pay.

Connor looked to Simon, narrowing his eyes at him. "Did she recognize you?"

Simon looked at Connor and scrunched his eyebrows. "No, boss, I don't think she did."

"You better fucking hope she didn't, you fucking idiot," Connor growled.

Simon remained by the door and listened.

Jake looked between the two men. He didn't know what the men were talking about. "What the fuck, man?" he asked Simon.

"I killed the girl's mother," he answered simply and

shrugged.

"Are you fucking kidding me?" Jake growled. "You didn't think to tell me that before I took you with me?"

"And miss out on the fun? Fuck no." Simon grinned.

"Enough!" Connor yelled. "Well, where are they?" Connor looked between the two men.

Simon looked up to the ceiling, and Jake leaned down and put his head in his hands.

Connor chugged the rest of his whiskey down and slammed the glass down on the table beside him. "Will someone please tell me what the fuck is going on?"

Jake finally looked up at his father, knowing his father's anger was coming for him next. "They outsmarted us; they're home at Jennifer's place right now."

Connor's breathing increased, and he clenched his fists tightly. "You mean to tell me the girl saw Simon and you let them get the fuck away?" His voice rose with each syllable he spoke. He stood and began to pace the floor in front of Jake.

"We will fix it, don't worry." Jake looked to Simon for reassurance and back to his father. "Relax, we got this."

Connor stopped right in front of Jake and grabbed him by the front of his shirt. He pulled him up face-to-face with him. "Relax? You got this?" he spat out. "I should fucking shoot you and go take care of this myself. Do you realize what that girl could do to us? You are a fucking failure just like your brother. For fuck's sake." Connor released one hand, pulled back, and punched Jake in the jaw.

Jake fell back into the chair. The sudden pain in his jaw was nothing unusual from a hit from his father. He knew it was coming. His father didn't tolerate screw-ups. He wasn't normally on the end of the fist, though. It was usually Sean taking the hit. It was definitely not a nice feeling.

Connor walked over to the bar and poured himself another whiskey and stood firm. The anger poured off of him. Taking a few deep breaths, he then turned. "Both of you get the fuck out of here. Fix your fuckup and don't come back until it is done." Connor grabbed his drink and left the den.

Jake wiggled his jaw to make sure it didn't get stiff and looked to Simon. "Well, I guess the rules go out the window." Failure my ass, Jake thought.

Simon grinned. "Let's do it."

Chapter Twenty-Four

Jenn woke to extreme warmth flowing through her body and a throb between her legs. The sensation felt incredible; she didn't want to open her eyes, but she did. She had to know what was causing such an amazing feeling. Feeling more awake, she could feel more of what was going on. She felt a tingle and moaned. She lifted the blanket to see Sean's head between her legs, his mouth pressed to her exposed pussy. He was licking it like it was the tastiest thing around.

Her hips instinctively flexed up, her body wanting more. She heard Sean chuckle. She bit her lip and accepted everything he was giving her.

Sean licked, nipped, and sucked. "You like that, babe?" He slipped a finger in her warm channel and slid it out. Pushing his finger inside of her, he clamped his lips around her swollen nub and sucked.

"Ahhhh." Jenn's back arched off the bed. She was getting close, but didn't want this feeling to end. The things he did to her body were something she never wanted to ever let go.

"Let it go, Babe. Just let go." Sean sank two fingers into her wet pussy and curled the ends, rubbing along her sweet spot.

She couldn't hold it any longer. Her toes curled, her tummy tightened, everything in her in her screamed for her to release. When Sean's finger hit that most sensitive spot deep inside of her, she had no control left. She exploded. "Sean…" She screamed. Her body spasmed from head to toe while he licked and fingered every drop from her, until she was limp.

He pulled his face and fingers from her wet pussy and crawled up her naked body, lavishing her with wet kisses along the way. He got to her breasts and suckled each before reaching Jenn's mouth.

Even though she was satiated from her explosive orgasm, she wanted more. She always wanted more from him. She would take everything and then some. Every spot he kissed or touched tingled. She could feel his erection rub along her leg, and she shivered at what she knew he could do to her with it. His lips met hers, and she took them with a need she would always have for him.

Sean slipped his tongue into her mouth, sliding it against hers. He sucked and nibbled on her lips while caressing her smooth skin from hip to breast. He shifted his pelvis to line up with hers, and when his hard cock hit her wet opening, he groaned. Jenn lifted her hips and he pushed forward. Thrusting his erection into her warmth, he released her mouth and cursed. "Fuck, the feeling just gets better and better." He cupped her breast with one hand and teased her nipple while holding himself up with the other. He pulled his cock out to the tip and pushed back in, harder and faster.

Jenn reached her arms around to his back, sliding her hands down to his ass, encouraging him for more. Every thrust sent shivers through her, he seemed to touch every nerve ending inside her. "Harder," she moaned.

Each time he plunged, Jenn moaned in pleasure and her hips bucked to meet him thrust for thrust. She was loving it. A demanding rhythm started between them.

Sean's hands gripped her hips; he pulled her even closer.

With the way Sean held her, the way they moved, Jenn could no longer keep her hold. Loving the sensations she was feeling with him being so deep inside of her, she took hold of the sheets and took what was being given. Never had Sean been this deep, this close, and she loved it. She wanted harder, and he gave it. She agreed with him; it seemed to get better and better. Her mouth was getting dry from her heavy panting and moaning. She licked her lips. "Holy fuck, Sean! That feels amazing." Meeting him thrust for thrust, she didn't think she would last much longer. He hit her sweet spot every time. She already came once, she didn't know how her body would handle another.

Sean moved one hand to her clit and began to rub it.

Her skin was beyond flush. She knew she was about ready to blow.

He must of seen the signs, because he began to rub her clit more and began to pump harder and faster. "Fucking let it go, Jenn, I am going to blow." He thrust once, twice—"Right fucking, now!"—three times and shouted out his release while he slammed one final time into her.

She tensed, and it felt like a full-body explosion happened. The biggest orgasm she ever had took hold of her, and her body shook and spasmed for, what felt like, forever. She bit her lip, trying not to scream too loud, and she squeezed her eyes tight until her body began to relax. "Holy shit, that was intense." She opened her eyes to see Sean's dark gray eyes peering down at her. She smiled.

"Yes, it was. You okay, babe?"

"Never better."

Sean slid his cock out of her warmth and rolled to his side to lay with her. He pulled the blanket up to cover them. He leaned on his elbow facing her and laid his other hand on her stomach. "I love you, Jenn. You know that?"

Jenn looked at him and smiled. "I do. I love you, too. You know that?"

Sean returned the smile. "I do."

They laid there in silence just staring at each other for a few moments, basking in the afterglow. "So, when do we start the plan?" Sean asked.

Jenn chewed on her cheek for a moment. She wished she could erase the shitstorm they were in and just live happily ever after, but she knew they couldn't. They didn't live in a fairy tale. She needed to help Sean gain back control of his life, and she wanted people to pay for her mother's death. She had thought long and hard, and if that payback included her own father, then so be it. "Let's get showered, eat, and then we'll start."

Chapter Twenty-Five

It was eleven o'clock in the morning when Sean got out of the shower. He walked into the kitchen to see Jenn looking through the file he gave her. It was his father's file, full of information and details that would hopefully help them in the case against him. When his father gave him the file, he surely didn't think his own son would turn on him, so now, with any luck, the information would be of good use.

There was information in the file that didn't need to be in there. It was as if his father kept scrap papers with details and just tossed it in and never threw anything out. Inside were pictures dating back from when Jenn was a kid. It disgusted him to know that his father had been keeping tabs on her for that long.

When he got the file from his father he never really went through it all, he just skimmed the top page, the most recent piece of info, and listened to his father speak. With the spread Jenn had on the table—receipts from her mortgage, information about her ex-boyfriend, even pictures of the fucker—it made him ill. To know that his father had no boundaries for his bullshit revenge literally made him sick. If he had known how bad his father really was, he would have taken Jenn from the get-go and ran three years ago.

Jenn must have heard him come into the room. She looked up from the mess on the table.

Sean noticed the glint in her eyes. He was only wearing a pair of faded jeans that rode low on his hips and by the look she was giving, he must have looked damn good.

"Hey," she said as she licked her lips.

"Hey, back." He leaned down and kissed those newly wet lips.

"Your father is a very sick man," she said and turned her attention back to the clutter on the table.

"He sure is. I never realized how bad. I am sorry." He moved around to sit in the chair next to her.

"It's not your fault, Sean. Look at all this shit. Not once did I know I was being followed." She picked up a picture of herself that showed her sitting at a café having lunch, and sighed.

"If I had known all this shit was going on, I swear I would never have let it get this far." Sean reached his hand up and grabbed her closest hand.

Jenn gave him a small smile. "And how would you have done that, hmm?"

"Kidnapped you earlier and ran." He chuckled, trying to make light of the situation.

Jenn shook her head at him. "It's okay, Sean. With this file maybe we can nail his ass to the ground, and he won't see a speck of daylight for a long time."

Sean dropped his head to the table, letting it thump with a bang. The guilt he was feeling after seeing all the intel his father had was eating him alive. He looked back up at her. "He has a lot of friends in high places."

Jenn sat up straight in her chair. "Now you listen here, mister. We are not defeated, yet. Your father is a bastard, and he is going to pay. I just happened to make a phone call while you were in the shower."

Sean was curious. He sat up straight and looked at her. "Who?"

"I called my father back." She raised her eyebrows. "I told him that if and when the police got involved, and he didn't confess to what he knew, that he was dead to me. That he would never see or hear from me ever again, and he would never meet or see his grandchildren. If he ever has any."

Sean was shocked that she would make that call. He had thought she was done with her father already, but then again, James was the only family she had. "What did he say?"

"He told me he was sorry for everything, and if he could take everything back, he would. He said he would do whatever it took to keep his family." She began to gather the papers and photos on the table to put back into the folder.

"That's it?"

"Yep."

"So what's he going to do?" He helped gather the papers and looked at her.

"I don't know really. I guess we will have to wait and see." She put the papers in the folder, closed it, and set it in front of her.

"All right then. So now we wait?" He questioned her.

"Yep. Let your brother and Simon come to us. They know we're here. I will call the police and get the ball rolling." She grinned.

Sean really hoped her plan worked out and no one got hurt. Jenn getting hurt was the last thing he wanted.

Chapter Twenty-Six

Sean knew a little bit about his brother. Knowing that he was human too is what allowed them the time to sleep. Knowing that he would have to regroup during daylight hours is what allowed them to relax during the day. His brother proved him right. Jenn and Sean were curled up on the couch watching an early evening movie, when Sean noticed a shadow creep by the window beside the TV. He gave Jenn a little body squeeze. "Jenn," he whispered.

Jenn yawned. "Yeah?"

Sean shifted on the couch. "I think they're here." He turned the TV off with the remote.

She turned her head to face him. "Let's do this," she said with excitement in her voice.

Sean chuckled at Jenn's excitement. His fierce woman ready to fight. He hadn't seen her like that before and it was hot. He liked that side of her. Sean noticed another shadow pass by the window. He knew both men were there and it was time. "Grab the phone and head to your room." Taking charge of the situation, he instructed Jenn what to do.

She rolled her eyes. "Whatever." She grabbed the portable phone and headed toward her bedroom.

"Don't think I didn't see that eye roll, babe." He laughed, shaking his head. "This was your plan." He went to his bag to grab his gun. He checked to see that it was loaded and shoved it in the back of his pants. He didn't plan to use it, but if he had to, he would.

He heard the door knob jiggle. He knew the doors were locked, but Jake knew how to pick them. Sean stalked over to the bathroom and slipped in. No lights were on, and he wanted to try and keep that to his advantage. Jenn's house was not big, and the layout was simple, but in the dark, you could trip over anything and everything that got in your way.

Sean heard the front door open; it creaked since the hinges needed oiling. Keeping as quiet as he could, he wait and listened. Two sets of footsteps entered. He tried to peek through the crack of the door to see what was happening, but all he could see was shadows. Then he heard whispers.

"They must be sleeping," Jake whispered.

Simon quietly moved further into the room. "That makes it easier for us." He looked around.

Jake advanced further into the room, bumping into a table. "Fuck," Jake gritted under his breath. "It's so damn dark in here, how the hell are you walking around in here and not hitting anything?" he whispered, pain clearly evident.

"I am taking my time and feeling my way around, you jackass," Simon grumbled.

Sean heard them move farther into the room and closer to the bedroom. He needed to distract them. He had tested the bathroom door earlier in the day to see if it squeaked, and it didn't, so he was safe. He looked around the dark room, glancing from shadow to shadow to see what he could toss. There was a cup on the vanity. It was plastic so he felt that was good enough. He eased the door open and tossed it out a little ways and listened for the slight thump as it hit the ground.

Jake turned around. "What was that?"

Simon pulled his gun from the back of his pants. "Someone knows we are here." Simon spoke casual.

"What?" Jake whispered.

"Oh, cut the crap, you idiot. You can't be that stupid. Your brother knows we're here."

"Yo, Sean. Why don't you come on out, bro," Jake shouted.

Sean stood in the bathroom listening to the fools in the living room. Should he leave his hiding place and go face them, or pray the police showed up before someone got hurt? He didn't know Simon that well, but he knew he wasn't a patient man. With hopes that the police were quick, he opened the bathroom door, and with his gun raised, he stepped out.

The clouds shifted at just the right time, allowing the moon to shine in the windows. Just enough light shone in to make out each person placed in the room and who had what in their hands. Sean noted that Simon had a gun raised and was heading toward the bedroom. Jake was just standing there and was empty-handed. "Simon, stop right there." He cocked the gun in warning.

Simon stopped in his tracks and turned. He kept his gun raised and pointed in Sean's direction. "Brave little fucker, aren't you?"

"This shit is going to end here. And it is going to end now," Sean growled.

Jake stood there. He looked between the two men as if watching a tennis match. Shaking his head, he reached around to the back of his pants and pulled his gun out. He cocked it and pointed it at Sean. "What the fuck, man? Why you go turning on us?"

"Seriously, Jake?" Sean gritted out. "Grow a fuckin' pair and open your eyes. This isn't our war. It's Dad's. Too many innocent people have been killed or are being killed."

"Oh, poor baby has grown a conscience." Simon laughed.

"And, you, motherfucker, are just as bad as our father." Sean looked to Jake. "You do realize, Jake, that if you didn't complete your job, dear ol' Simon here would have killed you, too?" He looked back to Simon for confirmation.

Simon shrugged. "It's just business."

Jake looked at Sean, then at Simon. "Simon knows I would complete my job, unlike some useless piece of shit like you," Jake taunted.

Sean had to laugh. Jake was so blind, so corrupted by his father. He had been doing their father's bidding for so much longer than he, there was no help left for him now. He was a lost cause. "Suit yourself, Jake. Either way, you are all going to pay."

Simon cocked his gun, the sound loud enough for everyone in the room to hear. He narrowed his eyes, aimed the gun, and fired.

Sean tried to move, but he wasn't fast enough. He was hit, and it hurt like a son of a bitch. His body jolted to the left, and he almost lost his balance. Without dropping his gun, he grabbed his injured arm and applied pressure, growling in pain. "Fuck!" Blood dripped down his arm. He heard a muffled scream come from the bedroom and hoped that Jenn wouldn't come out and get in harm's way.

Sean returned fire at Simon but missed. He heard the bullet ricochet off what he assumed was the table lamp and hit a wall somewhere. He was normally a good shot, but with trying to stop himself from bleeding out and worrying about Jenn, his aim just plain sucked. He heard Simon chuckle as he backed up against the wall to hold himself up, never lowering his gun or his eyes from the men both aiming at him.

He noticed Jake moving closer to the bedroom. Not wanting him to get any closer, he directed his aim at his brother and fired. He managed to hit Jake in one of his legs and watched his brother stumble to the ground. "Stay the fuck down, Jake, or I will shoot again," Sean yelled out.

"Saving me a part of my job." Simon snickered and peered over at Jake bleeding on the floor by the bedroom. He shook his head and looked back at Sean and moved closer to him. As he moved, he yelled, "Oh, little girl. If you want your brave boyfriend here to live, I would get out here right the fuck now!" Simon cocked his gun again.

The bedroom door opened slowly, and Sean noticed her trembling body standing in the doorway. "Stay there, Jenn. Don't come any closer." Sean looked at Jake and saw he was more concerned about his bleeding leg than the situation evolving in the room. Which worked out well in Jenn's favor. He noticed her look down at Jake and then back at Simon and then him. In the moonlight he saw the tears streaming down her face.

"Get over here, bitch, or I will shoot him again!" Simon yelled "Now!" and aimed the gun at Sean.

Sean squeezed his eyes tight. This was not how he wanted it to play out. He opened his eyes and noticed that Jenn was moving. He looked right at her and shook his head. He didn't want her any closer.

Simon looked back at Sean then back toward Jenn. He moved his firing arm off to the right just a smidgen and fired.

Sean ducked to the left, and Jenn screamed.

"That is the last warning you get, bitch. Now get the fuck over here."

Sean noticed out of his peripheral vision that Jake seemed to have come to his senses. He repositioned himself on the floor and beginning to take aim. He hoped that Jake would aim at him, but Jake was taking aim at Jenn. "Jenn, get down!" Sean yelled.

Suddenly, the front door burst open. "Put your guns down and your hands up. We have you surrounded." That was when everyone noticed the flashing blue and red lights outside. Several police officers stormed into the house as each man lowered their weapon.

Sean lowered his gun as the commotion began and thanked the lord that the police had arrived. He didn't get a chance to move far before Jenn was suddenly wrapping him in her arms and checking him for injuries. He felt her hands on his arm, and he winced. He gritted through the pain. He just barely heard her tell the police that they need to call the paramedics. Between the pain and Jenn's warm body, even though it was trembling and she was crying, he was thankful to be alive.

Chapter Twenty-Seven

Down at the police station, Sean and Jenn watched as Jake and Simon were booked for breaking and entering, attempted murder, and holstering nonregistered weapons. They were placed in separate cells with a bail hearing set for the next day.

They were then placed in an interrogation room after Sean refused to go to the hospital. They sat in uncomfortable chairs, but at least they had a table to lean on. Sean's arm was bandaged and in a sling. Jenn knew she would have to get him to the hospital afterward.

Sean appeared to be getting drowsy from the pain meds he received from the paramedics. The detective finally decided to make his appearance after making them wait nearly twenty minutes. Sean looked at the man, to Jenn, then adjusted his sling.

"It's quite the coincidence that this all was happening this evening, Miss Samos," the detective stated. "We have had a James Samos at the precinct all afternoon, spilling his guts on all illegal affairs unknown to mankind about those two men we locked up."

Jenn felt herself blush. She was happy her father came to his senses and became the man she always knew he was.

"I am glad he finally confessed."

The detective looked to Sean. "Mr. Samos had plenty to say about a Connor Green, as well. I would be correct to assume that would be your father?" He questioned.

Sean nodded. "Yes, sir."

"One of my officers mentioned that you had a file for me to look at?"

Jenn handed him the folder and placed her hands in her lap. "This is everything Connor had on me. He has been watching me, setting me up, and recently put a hit on me because I witnessed my mother's murder."

The detective opened the folder and began to sift through the paperwork. He sat back in his chair and scratched what looked like three-day-old scruff. He looked up at the pair sitting in front of him. "With this information alone we can get a warrant for Connor's arrest, and with your father's confession he can be looking at prison time for the murder of your mother and so much more."

"And what about the other men?" Jenn asked.

He leaned forward, setting his arms on the table. "Well, considering the one gentleman you call Simon, otherwise known as Carl, otherwise known as Robert, is wanted in three other states for several illegal affairs, I can't see him going too far. And as for your brother—" He looked at Sean. "With everything he has done for your father, according to Mr. Samos, he is also looking at a hefty prison time."

Jenn and Sean both nodded.

Jenn didn't really want to ask, but she needed to know. She didn't want to lose him now that she had him. She looked to Sean and could see fear in his eyes. He knew he was going to do time as well since he wasn't innocent. She cleared her throat. "What about Sean? He helped gather the intel, and he saved me. Is there anything that you can do to help him?" She bit her lip and prayed that the detective would help.

The detective looked between the two and sprouted a wide grin. "Well, you see. Mr. Samos didn't mention Sean in anything. And there is no proof Sean did anything but defend himself." He sat back in his chair, crossed his legs, and put his hands in his lap. "So in mine, and in any officer's eyes in this precinct, he is a free man."

Sean looked at Jenn with shock in his eyes, then back at the detective. "Seriously?" He had to ask.

"I haven't been more serious in my life, son. And if anything comes to light in our investigation, I don't see any reason not to just toss it in the trash. That is, unless there is something you need to tell me?" He looked right at Sean.

Sean swallowed and licked his lips. "No, sir, I'm good. Thank you."

"All right then. Why don't you take the pretty lady and head on home. If we have any questions we will call. You both will be safe from now on, and if you need anything, don't hesitate to call me personally." He reached into his front pocket and pulled out a card and handed it to them. "By the way, young lady, I knew your mother when we were both just teenagers." He winked, shook both their hands, and left the room.

Sean looked at Jenn and blew out a breath. "We did it." He smiled at her. He stood up and pulled her up with his good arm and hugged her. He pressed his lips to her's, giving her a deep, passionate kiss, and then pulled back. "Let's go get me checked out, and then go home." He took her hand in his. They walked out of the room and the precinct together.

Epilogue

Three months later…

Sean woke to the sound of puking coming from the bathroom. Jenn had mentioned not feeling well the night before and had gone to bed early, so he didn't think anything of it. But now she was puking. He tossed the blankets aside and got up from the bed. He walked to the bathroom and opened the door. The sight he walked into broke his heart. Poor Jenn was sprawled on the floor gripping the toilet seat, and she was white as a ghost. "Ah, shit, Jenn, are you okay?"

Jenn heard him, but couldn't respond with words. When she went to speak, vomit came out instead. Leaning up into the toilet, she retched the remaining bile from her stomach and groaned.

"You are sick, babe. What can I do?" Sean moved into the bathroom and grabbed a washcloth. He wet it and placed it on the back of her neck. He kneeled down beside her and began to rub her back.

"I think I'm dying." Jenn groaned again.

Sean chuckled. "You probably have the flu, babe. Let me help you." He reached his arms around her legs and shoulders and lifted her up. He curled her close to his body and carried her to the bedroom. He laid her on the bed and covered her up. Kissing her on the forehead, he left to go get a glass of ginger ale and a puke bowl.

In the kitchen, he thought back to when Jenn was taking care of him, changing the bandages on his gunshot wound. The looks she would give at the sight of the blood. The poor woman. She would turn green and pale in color. They had come a long way in the past three months. Making up the time he had missed, trying to make up for his wrongs. Putting his father and brothers behind bars and getting to know one another again was a blessing. It had been a slow process, but he would do it all again to be with her. She was his life. He loved her and always would. He grabbed a bowl and poured some ginger ale.

He returned to the room and found Jenn fast asleep. She looked so pale lying there on the white sheets. He wished he could take her illness away. He set the drink on the bedside table and the puke bowl on the floor beside her. After walking around to his side of the bed, he sat on the edge.

He opened the drawer to his table and took out the black velvet case that was inside. He had plans for the evening, but with Jenn not well, he wasn't sure if he was going to carry them out in the same way. He opened the case and looked at the beautiful platinum full-carat princess diamond ring and smiled to himself. He was finally free. He got his girl and he was free. He had never been so happy in his life. He closed the case and put it back in the drawer. He sat back on the bed and rested his head against the headboard, closing his eyes just to rest. He wanted to be easily wakened if Jenn needed him.

***

It was early afternoon when Jenn woke again, and she

was feeling much better. She had news to tell Sean and him catching her throwing up didn't seem to give him any hints. She stretched her aching body and sat up in bed. She looked over at Sean; she didn't expect to see him in bed still. "Hey, thanks for the help this morning."

Sean closed the laptop he was playing Candy Crush on. He set the computer on the stand beside the bed. "Anything for you, babe. Are you feeling better?"

"Much better, thank you."

"That's good. It must have been a twenty-four-hour bug or something." He leaned into her and kissed her forehead.

"Or something," she mumbled. She didn't know how to tell him. She was on birth control for so long, that when she switched to the injection, she completely forgot about having to go back every few months. And with all the commotion with the kidnapping and all, the injection date flew by, and she and Sean had had unprotected sex… It wasn't until she realized that she hadn't had a period for two months that it dawned on her, and she went and got tested. Now she had to tell him, especially since the symptoms had progressed and she might start showing any day now.

"What was that?"

Jenn took a deep breath. She had to tell him. He was going to find out. She was actually surprised he hadn't noticed her breasts. They had been extra sensitive lately. She took his hand in hers and looked him in the eye. "Sean, you know I love you, right?"

Sean narrowed his eyes and slowly answered. "Yes."

"And I wouldn't plan anything without consulting you first." She bit her lip, trying to hold her tears at bay. It was so hard to tell him this. She didn't know how he was going to react.

"Where you going with this, Jenn?" He squeezed her hand.

"I'm pregnant," she whispered and closed her eyes.

"Stop mumbling, Jenn, and speak up."

Jenn opened her eyes and saw the sparkle in his eyes. She wasn't sure if he was joking or not until she saw the wide grin across his face. "You bastard." She grabbed a pillow and smacked him with it. "So you're happy about this?"

"Fuck yeah, I am! Please say it again, just once, please," he begged.

Jenn sighed. Relieved that he was happy, but still scared for the future. "I am pregnant. There, happy?"

Sean jumped toward her, tackling her on the bed. "I sure fucking am. You are having my baby." He began to tickle her and nuzzle her neck.

"Sean, stop. Stop, Sean, I am going to pee." She laughed.

Sean stopped and sat up in the bed. "There is only one more thing that would make this the best day of my life." He turned toward the nightstand, opened the drawer, and took out the little black velvet case. He turned toward Jenn and handed it to her.

Jenn's laughter instantly stopped. She looked down at the case and back up at Sean. "What's this?"

"Open it."

Jenn opened the black box to the most exquisite ring she had ever seen. She gasped. She could feel the tears build up in her eyes. Feeling the bed move, she looked at Sean who was now on the move. She watched his every movement.

Sean walked around to her side of the bed, got down

on bended knee, and reached for her hands. Once her hands were in his grasp, he began. "Jennifer, my beautiful Jenn. I have always hoped we would end up together. It may have taken us walking through hell to get here, but we made it. I don't ever want to let anything, or anyone, get in the way of our happiness again. I want to spend the rest of my days living free and happy with you and our children, knowing that my love was never wasted or lost to another. You are my 'one,' my only. Will you marry me?"

Tears streamed down her face, as her body trembled from emotional overload. She loved Sean with all her being. He was the only man she had ever loved and would ever love. Now she was carrying his child inside of her, and the past was behind them. They could finally build a future together. There was only one answer for him. "Yes!"

About the Author

Jean is just a small town girl looking for a little adventure. With her love of reading and writing she wanted to explore and see what her characters could do for her. Being a full-time nurse, wife, and mother of two boys, she has her hands full, but takes the time to dream among the pages. She is a true-blooded Canadian and hopes to explore parts of the world sometime in the future, but for now, she explores in the books she reads and writes. Being a huge indie author fan, she has made several friends online and has met a few at book signings. Hoping to one day meet some fans face-to-face, she would gladly friend you on Facebook, Goodreads, and Google+.

She can be found on:
Facebook: https://www.facebook.com/jean.kelso.14
Goodreads:
https://www.goodreads.com/author/show/8338589.Jean_
Kelso
Google+ as Barb Jean Kelso Johnson

www.ingramcontent.com/pod-product-compliance
Lightning Source LLC
Chambersburg PA
CBHW020133180626
46810CB00004B/1528

* 9 7 8 0 9 9 5 1 9 2 9 2 8 *